Miranda,
It's on the way.
Wait on it,
KaJackson
3/22/14

Love is a Journey

KIMBERLYN S. ALFORD

Rapier
PUBLISHING COMPANY

Love is a Journey
ISBN 978-0-9839483-1-5

Published by
Rapier Publishing Company
3417 Rainbow Parkway
Rainbow City, Alabama 35906
www.rapierpublishing.com

Printed in the United States of America

Book Design by: Delaney-Designs and Pete Pierce
Book Layout by: Delaney-Designs
Photography by: Ross Roddy

I refer to Love is a Journey as the third book in the Love Series but not because I'm thinking of romance but because of the presence of God's love, forgiveness, grace and mercy in the lives of these characters which depict what God has allowed me to experience as his child.

The Love Series includes: Free to Love Again, Love Covers All and now Love is a Journey.

DEDICATION

In Loving Memory Of

My Maternal Grandparents

Joseph Hezekiah Brown Wilson

May 18, 1886 – April 6, 1972

And

Susie Ceasar Wilson

October 8, 1906 – July 22, 2006

Aunt Bettye J. Moore Wilson

Aunt Ella Mae Gilbert

Uncle Aaron Antley

Christie Scott Blasingame

ACKNOWLEDGEMENTS

God our Father is faithful. Life brings about many challenges. One thing is certain God is always with us. Through the deepest pain, the most challenging tests God does not change. He is forever present, but because we are in the flesh, he allows us to share this life with others who remind us of His AWESOMENESS.

Thanks to my husband, Kevin. Thanks to my two wonderful children, my son, Corey Darnell, my eldest and my daughter, Rebekah Annette, my youngest. Thanks Mom (Mildred Wilson Corbitt), step-dad (Johnny Corbitt), and sisters (Gale Audrey, and Joy Delois). Thanks to my sisters in Christ - Debra and Cynthia. Thanks to my aunts and uncles (Auntie Queen, Auntie Eva, Aunt Odell, Aunt Valeria, Aunt Frances, Aunt Roxie and Uncle James). To all of my cousins – thanks for your support - keep moving forward. Valencia Pierce thanks for all of your prayers, encouragement and helping me come up with a title that fits this story.

Each person that we have the privilege of meeting in this lifetime has the potential to impact us in a positive way. I am grateful for all of those who have taken a few moments to shape my life by making small deposits of quality time and words of encouragement. Every laugh, smile, message, hug… made a difference in the way I moved forward. Because of all of you and who you are to me, I have been encouraged and will continue to seek God's true plan for my life.

Prologue

Marcie sat down in her living room and thought about the good things Anthony had brought to her life. He made her feel safe, desirable, and loved. Anthony was her knight in shining armor. He was the man whom all girls dream of meeting, but unfortunately for her – her past would not let go. Instead of him being her knight, Marcie felt like Anthony was too good to be true. She was afraid that Anthony had a dark side like David.

Marcie was determined not to make the same mistake again. Anthony seemed to be pushing towards a commitment, and she wasn't sure if she was ready to take that much of a chance. One thing Marcie was sure of was the fact that she enjoyed the peace and companionship she had when she was with Anthony. He never showed signs of anything but patience with her. Marcie hated the fact that she was so afraid. She hated what David had done to her psyche.

Chapter 1

David

David sat calmly on the bus stop bench waiting for the arrival of his bus. All he wanted to do was to get away from this place. No one understood. He was not that way anymore, and yet no one seemed to care. Even Marcie seemed out to get him. She had half of the jury in tears by the time she finished her testimony. The jury was deliberating but they were certainly going to convict him again. Marcie was convincing, and sadly telling the truth. He wasn't going to wait around for them to shackle him and escort him back into the dungeon. He wasn't sure where he was going, but he was not going back to jail. He boarded the bus at noon, and by 3 p.m. when the jury reconvened he was safely across the state line - headed nowhere hoping to get a fresh start.

Marcie, Anthony, Kent, Monique

The judge re-entered the courtroom and everyone stood for the verdict. It was 3:15 p.m. and David's attorney sat alone at the defendant's table.

Monique looked at Kent. Her eyes conveyed her concern. She whispered, "Where's David?" Kent looked at her directly trying to offer reassurance. "Maybe he's late or outside." He knew that wasn't going to fly, but he was hoping it would for Marcie's sake.

The absolute look of terror on Marcie's face as she starred at the empty seat once occupied by David told the true story. David was on the run, and her life was about to be turned upside down.

The judge allowed the verdict to be read in David's absence. He was guilty on all counts and now considered a convicted felon on the run. A warrant for his arrest was issued by the judge. Although the verdict was guilty, with David still on the loose, Marcie knew she wouldn't be sleeping through the night for a long time. Monique laid her head on Kent's shoulder and began to pray. Marcie put her head in her hands and began to sob. Anthony pulled her into his arms not knowing what else to do. Court was adjourned and as the room cleared the couples remained seated oblivious to the movement around them.

Minutes passed before Kent and Monique broke their embrace and stood up. Anthony's shirt was soaked with Marcie's tears. Monique knew that the best thing for Marcie was for her to get back home and back into her routine. She'd done her part now it was up to the authorities to find David and put him back in jail.

Chapter 2

David

David's mind began to wonder back to the night that proved to be his final act of violence against Marcie and the beginning of his torment as an incarcerated man. He learned that "wife beaters" became victims themselves once they entered prison. He had experienced more than his share of trips to the infirmary since arriving at Calhoun State Prison. One of his attackers "Big Jake" recounted to him the story of how his father beat his mother to death while he and his 3 year old brother watched as he pounded David's head into the cement wall. That beating resulted in David spending two weeks in the infirmary with a concussion and two broken ribs and another month in solitary confinement for his own safety.

David had a lot of time to think about that nearly fatal night. He remembered it so well. He had gone out after work with a couple of the guys to get a few drinks. A few drinks turned into six Heinekens and a few shots of vodka. On the way home he decided to use the last of his nickel bag from the night before. He'd recently started mixing alcohol and street drugs. It seemed harder for him to get a "high" lately so he'd decided to try other combinations.

By the time he reached the apartment he was anxious and on the edge. He'd gotten suspended from work because he had a loud disagreement with his supervisor. He really didn't want to hear Marcie's mouth so when she asked where he had been he did the first thing he could do to shut her up. He punched her in the mouth as hard as he could. He remembered yelling at her to stay down as he ran to the kitchen and grabbed one of the knives from the drawer. The next thing he remembered was being covered in blood, and Marcie was nowhere in sight. He only wished now that it was a dream. But it wasn't. He had almost killed Marcie. He knew now that it was only God that spared her life because his actions could have very well ended her time on earth.

David thought about how alcohol and drugs had helped him achieve the statistic status expected of minority males. He was determined to stay clean and reach out to other young men and hopefully help them avoid his terrible mistakes.

David's problems had begun long before he met Marcie. He'd been caught drinking and driving twice before he was old enough to drive, but his mother was friends with the district attorney's wife and seemed to always find a way to keep him out of the juvenile justice system. He never understood why his mother could get him out of trouble, but she couldn't help herself. He wished she had the courage to stand up to his father.

David's problems had continued into adulthood. He'd graduated high school and gone straight to work. His only goal was to get out of his father's house as soon as possible. He'd learned to avoid drinking and driving. When he met Marcie, he felt like his life was finally turning around but not long after he married Marcie the pressure of feeling he'd never be able to truly provide for her overwhelmed him and he began to drink daily again. He figured if he was intoxicated, he wouldn't have to face his shortcomings. The truth was – the more he drank – the more hopeless he felt. He was angry. His life had turned into the disaster his father had predicted and the only way he could deal with it was to drink more. Marcie though beautiful, reminded him of all that he was not. He didn't realize it then, but Marcie had truly loved him. She would have never walked out on him. He'd pushed her away. He'd destroyed their marriage – just as his father had predicted.

He thought back to the pain he saw in Marcie's eyes as she testified. He too had to suppress his own tears as he listened to Marcie talk about the way her mouth filled with blood after being punched by the man she thought loved her. She talked about feeling betrayed and feeling like her life would end right there. He had turned away when she recounted how he had slashed her side with the same kitchen knife she had used to slice the roast for that night's dinner. Blood had saturated her clothes and she had run from the apartment not knowing where she could go for help. She described how she barely made it to her sister before passing out and he realized he'd done that. He'd nearly killed a woman who had done nothing less than love him unconditionally. He gasped for his breath and tears began to stream down his cheeks as he realized that even though he was hours late, the table had been set when he got home that night and the oven was on keeping his dinner warm. Marcie was a good woman and he had treated her like crap. He could see so much clearer now and he wished that he could erase Marcie's pain. He wished she would forgive him but he knew he had no right to even ask that.

As the bus passed through miles of farm land, David continued to think about how he had gotten to this place. He knew it was because of his rebellious ways, which started when he was young. He'd chosen to do things his own way and now he'd never be a free man again; he'd also ruined Marcie' life. She still seemed as afraid, terrified even, as she was at the first trial. He could tell by the way Marcie spoke to the jury that she was still having sleepless nights. Time hadn't done much to heal her wounds and for that he was remorseful. Both of their lives were drastically altered and he had no one to blame, but himself.

David decided that his trip to nowhere would end at the next bus stop. He drifted off to sleep and two hours later he woke up. The name of the town seemed familiar, but he wasn't sure why. Maybe someone he'd met in prison had mentioned it. He wasn't sure, but something was very familiar about the name. He walked off of the bus hoping to find a new life. His own life had been full of abuse – as an adult and as a child. His father, when he was around, was always drinking and using him as a punching bag. He was the youngest and for some reason his father denied him as his son. That he never understood. As abusive as his father was to his mother, she would have been crazy to cheat on that demon. His mother was terrified of his father and didn't do anything to protect him when his father gave him his weekly "beat down". He remembered his father as being physically and verbally abusive - telling him he was "no good" and wouldn't amount to anything. So far he'd lived up to his father's expectations, but if there was a God in heaven, he was going to prove him wrong or die trying.

Chapter 3

Marcie and Anthony

Marcie could not believe all that happened earlier that day. She couldn't believe David would not be going to sleep in a jail cell where he belonged. Anthony refused to leave her side. The idea of knowing David was free made her physically and mentally sick. She made her way to the bathroom to throw up for the third time since she'd returned from court. She was scared, nervous, anxious and nauseated. Marcie wiped her face with a cold towel and then gargled with some mouth wash. As she walked back into the room, Anthony was nervously flipping through the channels. He noticed her and immediately turned to look at Marcie.

"I'm not going to lie." Anthony's voice was low and full of concern. "I don't know what to do. I'm worried about you." He paused and then began to walk towards Marcie. "I want you to know that I will not let David, hurt you again. I'm not going to let him get to you. You don't have to worry about that. He will make a mistake and get caught, but know that until he does I'll be a whisper away."

"I wish I didn't feel this way. I'm being controlled by fear and I don't know how to stop it." Marcie looked like she was carrying the weight of the world on her shoulders. Her eyes were swollen and red from crying and vomiting.

"I don't know when the fear will stop, but I know where to begin. Come here. Sit with me. Let's pray." Anthony took Marcie's hand and led her to a chair in the corner. He then kneeled in front of her and began to pray.

Marcie

After praying with Anthony and lying in his arms for what seemed like hours, which in actuality was only about twenty minutes, Marcie decided to freshen up. She walked into the bathroom once again and removed a towel from the shelf. As she allowed the water to run and get hot, she thought back to her testimony before the jury. David was her first love and only lover. She was a virgin when they married and no matter what he did, she couldn't shake her love for him. She couldn't imagine living without him until she realized that living with him could mean no life for her at all. He'd never gone that far before. She'd never seen him like that. He was out of control. If she hadn't run from the apartment, she was sure he would have killed her. Thinking back she didn't understand how "love" could be like that. Bruised ribs, black eyes…none of that was what she expected when she married David. She loved David with all of her heart and she really believed he loved her but when he was drinking he turned into a cruel and spiteful man. He was nothing like the man she fell in love with. The changes were gradual; however, had she not been so determined not to give up – determined not to quit she could have possibly avoided a lot of the pain she'd experienced at the hands of David.

When should she have drawn the line in the sand? Should she have walked away when he slapped her so hard that her contact popped out of her eye? Should she have left when he got angry and spit on her? Or maybe when he put her out of the car and told her to walk home? She felt like a failure. Why didn't she know that the day of total betrayal would soon come? Why didn't she know that David could possibly take her life? One thing she was certain of was that there had to be a God, because that's the only way she survived David's last outburst.

Marcie thought about how good it felt to have Anthony pray for her. Anthony seemed to be so peaceful even after losing his wife and having to be a single father. He seemed to take it all in stride and that made her determined to someday learn more about his God.

Marcie finished washing her face and rejoined her friend Monique who seemed eager to assess her state of mind and comfort her.

Monique and Marcie

Marcie, still shaken up about the day's event, with a heavy heart, walked slowly into the room. The minute she entered the room, Monique rushed to her side and gave her a hug.

"Marcie I know this isn't easy for you. I can understand some of the things that might be going through your mind. The only thing that I can tell you with certainty is that you have to keep moving forward. Fear can paralyze you if you let it and you've made too much progress to stop now."

Marcie knew that Monique had her best interest at heart. Monique was always positive – always looking ahead and so far – always right. She thought back on the first time she'd sought help at the battered women's shelter, Heart to Heart. Monique made it easy to ask for help. All of the ladies at the shelter looked up to her. Being on the run was a scary thing, but Monique made each of them feel safe. She let everyone know that operating the shelter was a passion for her not just a job. Somewhere along the way Monique had become a good friend. Marcie couldn't imagine where she'd be had she not met Monique.

Marcie nodded, but she did not speak. Slowly she lifted her eyes and looked at Monique dead on. "Monique, I appreciate your encouragement, but this time I can't help, but say it. You really don't know how it feels to fear for your life. Since the trial began I can't sleep. When I go to sleep at night, all I do is dream; and my dreams are never good. Some nights I dream of being shot, others of being choked, but it always ends the same – me lying there unconscious near death. I wake up in cold sweats wondering if someone is in my apartment – afraid to move – afraid of David all over again. You really don't know how it feels to fear for your life. You couldn't possibly understand how terrified I really am. – Everyday it gets worst." I can't get any rest because of these dreams. I need rest, but rest won't come.

Monique was caught off guard by Marcie's words: however, she was not at a loss for words. "Marcie, that's where you are wrong, I've worked with battered women and their children for almost fifteen years now. I've experienced a lot in my personal life, as well as. I've been threatened by the spouses of the women I have worked with and I was in an abusive relationship as well. I had an unstable fiancé of my own. I know from experience what it feels like to cry yourself to sleep praying that the night will end and hoping that you will wake up the next day. I know how embarrassing it can be to feel like your own weakness has landed you in a life threatening situation. I don't talk about it with my clients, because my service to them is not about me, but I need you to understand that there is hope. My ex-fiancé Michael was at the head of the class when it comes to abusers. I was a month short of making one of the biggest mistakes of my life – marrying Michael. Believe it or not that's how I got to know Kent. Michael turned into a stalker. He would break into my apartment when I was out. One time I came home and the smell of his cologne was still in my living room. I had to leave and go stay in a hotel for the night. Kent was the one who came to my rescue. He made sure I got out, filed a police report and then made it to work safely. For weeks I lived not knowing what Michael would do next. That's how Kent won my heart. He showed me a side of him that I didn't know existed. He showed me that chivalry was not dead. He confronted Michael on my behalf and refused to let me stay alone until he knew that Michael was no longer a threat. That was one of the scariest times of my life. At one point I moved in with Kent because I was afraid. This was long before I acknowledged how desirable he was. I was desperate. The truth is if it wasn't for Kent, my ex-fiancé Michael would have probably gone through with his plan to kill me. I know all too well how it feels to be afraid to go asleep at night Marcie, but I came to know how it feels to put myself first, how it feels to know that I have support and how it feels to move past the pain and enjoy my life. You have to choose to move forward Marcie. It won't be easy, but you can do it one day at a time."

"Monique you always seem so positive. This is one of the hardest things I've ever had to endure. Sometimes I want to just give up. I feel like burying my head in the sand. I've never been a hateful person. I've always avoided drama from my friends and arguments of any kind, but this has changed me. To be honest, I am so angry at David for turning my life upside down. He had a choice. If he didn't want to be with me, he could have walked away. Instead, it was like he set out to destroy me and I'm about one step away from hating him. I know hating another person isn't right, but what he did to me makes it hard for me to feel anything else. He left permanent scars – not just on my body, but he scarred my mind, my heart. I've changed in ways that I don't like. I cry for the woman David married because she's trapped inside this shell that refuses to be broken. She's trapped Monique and I can't get to her.

Sometimes I think if I could just get my licks back I'd feel better. If I could just kick his behind one good time, at least I wouldn't feel so helpless. I know it sounds crazy, but I'd love a chance to just pound on him for about five minutes. I wouldn't kill him but I sure would kick his behind with passion."

Monique couldn't help but grin. "Marcie you can't give up. This will get..." Monique was interrupted by Anthony as he walked into the room.

Anthony could tell by the tears in both Marcie and Monique's eyes that he had interrupted a serious conversation. Before he could speak Kent walked up behind him. Not wanting to make the situation any harder, he immediately turned facing Kent and spoke to him directly.

"Hey man let's go to the lobby and catch the end of the Redskin and Cowboys game. Last time the Redskins whipped the pants off the Cowboys."

Kent quickly glanced around the room his eyes hit Marcie first. Then, he quickly scanned Monique's face. Her expression told the entire story. This was not a good time. He and Anthony had definitely interrupted something. He gave his wife a reassuring smile and back peddled out of the room with Anthony urging him on.

Monique continued her thought as if they had never been interrupted. Taking Marcie by her hands, "Marcie, please listen. I know you can't believe me now, but I promise you this will get better. One day you will be able to let go of it all and just trust God to protect you. Your life is in God's hands you know. David can't do anything to you that God doesn't allow. I know that sounds like an indictment against God, but it isn't. As I reflect on all of the hard times I have experienced over the years, I have come to understand that each of them shaped me into the woman I am today. I have much room for improvement, but one thing is certain my trials have made me strong. They also revealed to me a treasure that I had been overlooking for years – Kent. I'm not saying that trials will bring you a husband, but I do believe that when we experience hard times the end result can be positive... especially if we faint not! Remember how you told me that your apartment was your first real place on your own? The job you got after you completed your recovery was your first salaried position. All I want you to do Marcie is to believe. Believe that there is something good in store for you and trust God to protect you." Monique looked at Marcie as if she was waiting for her to respond and as if cued Marcie opened her mouth to speak.

"I want to believe and I want to trust, but I don't know how."

Monique smiled, "Wanting to believe is half the battle. Let's just start there. She reached for Marcie to give her another hug. Marcie cried, but this time she felt as if a huge weight had been lifted from her shoulders.

Chapter 4

Anthony

Anthony packed the last box of the girls' clothes. The movers were set to arrive in two hours and he had not begun to get his own things together. When he and Rachel chose to make their home in Bald Knob, Arkansas, he couldn't imagine what it would be like to live in any other state. Now, all he could think about was being close to Marcie.

Anthony sat on the side of his bed thinking back to when he first met Marcie. He had been sitting in a booth at Jay's Cups and Books enjoying his favorite cup of hot chocolate, debating whether or not he should add more to the last article he had written when he noticed Marcie struggling to get her umbrella open. He had not noticed how beautiful she was before when she was sitting at the table with her friends, but suddenly he felt compelled to go introduce himself. He'd quickly rose from his seat and hurried to Marcie's side picking up the books she had dropped in her efforts to get her umbrella open. He was even more captured when she returned his kindness with a hypnotic smile. *That smile could get him to do anything. That smile was part of the reason he was packing up and moving to a new city and state. He wanted to spend the rest of his life with that smile.* After introducing himself, he asked if she'd like to have a cup of hot chocolate while he pretended to work hard to repair her umbrella.

He figured the harder he appeared to work on her umbrella, the more likely she'd be to see him again, but Marcie had not fallen for that scheme. Behind her beautiful smile was a 12 foot wall and she wasn't letting anyone in without a thorough interrogation. Initially, he wasn't even sure he had the energy to climb it, but he was so glad he had. His sense of humor and Marcie's smile were destined to find each other.

When Rachel died of pancreatic cancer, he thought he'd never love again. One day they were planning the rest of their lives together and the next day he was carrying her to the shower to give her a bath and trying to convince her that eating wouldn't make her sick "this time". It had been so hard watching his once independent, energetic, always on the go wife suffering daily. In the end, she depended on him for all of her daily needs. She was so weak and always in pain, yet always thinking about him and the girls. He missed Rachel so much. He couldn't imagine that ever changing. She'd given him so much, but she was gone and he had to live.

He was determined to take care of Marcie and to make sure David didn't do anything else to harm her. The condo he'd leased was perfect for now. The six month lease would give him an opportunity to decide which area of the city he wanted to purchase their new home. He hoped that in that time Marcie would also warm up to the idea of making a more permanent commitment.

Regardless of the outcome, he was sure that this move was the fresh start that he and the girls needed. Not only would he be there for Marcie, but he'd also have the support of his family, Kent and Monique. This would be a good move for everyone.

Anthony paused for a moment and looked around the master suite. He had enjoyed some of the best years of his life in this house. Rachel was a jewel. He sat on the side of the bed and slowly looked through the things that belonged to his widow. He finally had the courage to donate them to charity. Rachel had left him detailed instructions, but he'd delayed following through with them. Now, was the "right time" that Rachel mentioned in her journal. She'd always have a place in his heart, but now he understood what she meant about moving forward. Marcie was the woman Rachel had prayed for him to meet and in time he was certain he'd be able to convince her that marriage was intended to be a blessing from God not a prison sentence. He knew that Marcie was carrying a lot of baggage from her relationship with David, but he was willing to help her lighten her load.

Marcie

Marcie paced back and forth. She was excited, yet also scared. Excited that Anthony would be arriving later that afternoon, scared that David would find her and make good on his final threat to see her dead or die trying, she was an emotional train wreck.

Marcie couldn't help but wonder once again how her life became so chaotic. She remembered the David she fell in love with. Besides being handsome, he had a great sense of humor. The day they first met he'd spent twenty minutes telling her jokes and finally when she was laughing so hard that tears had begun to fall down her cheeks, he asked her to go on a date. The first few weeks had been like a dream. They stayed up all night talking. He did seem a little possessive but she liked the attention. Thinking back his possessiveness was probably the red flag she missed. He made her feel so special. He didn't pressure her. Being a virgin was never an issue with David. He always showed an interest in getting to know what was important to her.

Marcie emerged from her thoughts to the sound of the jazz CD Anthony gave her. It filled the apartment. She'd been listening to it every day for the last two weeks. Anthony promised to return as soon as possible and so far he'd kept all of his promises. His phone call earlier that morning was not a surprise. The surprise was that he'd actually been driving since midnight and was stopping to sleep for a couple of hours. He expected to arrive around 7 p.m. Marcie promised to meet him at the condo even though she'd barely been out of her apartment three times in the last two weeks. That included her trip to the grocery store this morning to buy a few things so that Anthony and the girls would have food and toiletry items when they arrived.

Monique insisted that Marcie allow her to pick her up for church two days before and she'd gone to the doctor for her annual checkup on Friday; and that was all. Unfortunately, she was almost out of leave time and she would have to return to work at the end of the week.

Knowing that Anthony would be just a phone call away was reassuring. He seemed so eager to take care of her. More important than his eagerness was the fact that he knew what to do when she was discouraged. He could always make her feel his presence regardless of how alone she felt. Anthony made her want to believe in true love. His friendship, kindness, and presence almost made her forget the pain of her past with David. She wanted to forget, but the truth was David was free and capable of almost anything.

Marcie sat down in her living room and thought about the good things Anthony had brought to her life. He made her feel safe, desirable, and loved. Anthony was her knight in shining armor. He was the man that all girls dream of meeting, but unfortunately for her – her past would not let go. Instead of him being her knight, Marcie felt like Anthony was too good to be true. She was afraid that Anthony had a dark side like David.

Marcie was determined not to make the same mistake again. Anthony seemed to be pushing towards a commitment and she wasn't sure if she was ready to take that much of a chance. One thing Marcie was sure of was the fact that she enjoyed the peace and companionship she had when she was with Anthony.

He never showed signs of anything but patience with her. Marcie hated the fact that she was so afraid. She hated what David had done to her psyche.

Anthony and Marcie

Anthony and Marcie sat in front of the fireplace after they finished getting Maxine and Mavis dressed for bed. The girls were excited about having their own rooms.

Marcie was glad to have Anthony near. The television was on, but neither of them watched. They sat quietly enjoying the moment. Anthony reached over and took Marcie's hand. Then, he broke the silence. "How have you been, Marcie? I missed you and I came back as soon as I could. I meant it when I said David will not hurt you again." He looked into Marcie's eyes and realized that she was more afraid than he'd imagined.

"Marcie I want you to stay with us tonight. You stay in my room and I'll sleep on the couch – it's a hide-a-bed."

Marcie opened her mouth to decline Anthony's offer and then she thought about how afraid she'd been for the last two weeks. She'd had to get sleeping pills when she went to the doctor, because she had not been sleeping more than two hours a night.

She looked at Anthony and smiled. Thinking that she was about to refuse, Anthony spoke up. "I know you have not been getting a lot of rest lately and I want you to feel safe. You need to get some rest."

"Thanks Anthony. I've only slept a couple of hours since the trial. I accept your offer. I have to go back to work the day after tomorrow and I'm going to need all the rest I can get."

"Thank you for not fighting me." He kissed her lightly on the forehead and continued. "The girls seemed almost as excited as I was to see you. I was happy to see that because they really like you. It was hard on them when Rachel died, but they are adjusting well. And with you in the picture, it's getting better."

Marcie smiled back at Anthony hoping her smile would be enough, but he wasn't going to let her off that easy. "What are you thinking about?"

Marcie hesitated, then, began to speak slowly. "Maxine and Mavis are beautiful. You are doing a wonderful job with them. That is evidenced by the way they carry themselves. They did seem happy to see me, but I wouldn't have expected anything else considering their father adores me." She winked and leaned into Anthony's waiting arms.

"Indeed, he does." Anthony replied. "Would you like a snack before bedtime?"

"Sure, how about some fruit? I think there's some cantaloupe and honeydew melon."

"I was thinking more like some chocolate covered strawberries."

"That sounds good, but I didn't buy strawberries."

Anthony smiled, "I never make promises I can't keep." He walked over to the cooler he'd brought in with him from the car and pulled out a carton of strawberries. He walked into the kitchen and returned fifteen minutes later with the chocolaty treats.

Marcie smiled as Anthony poured her half a glass of wine, "Hopefully, you'll be able to relax and get some well-deserved rest."

"Thanks Anthony. I feel relaxed just being in your presence."

Anthony walked to the back room. He emerged twenty minutes later with a pillow and blanket.

"The bed is made and I put towels and soap in the master bathroom. I also had an extra toothbrush it's on the counter. I'd love to talk to you until morning, but I'd rather know that you had a good night's sleep.

Marcie finished her wine and said goodnight.

Anthony smiled in response and then added, "Sleep late. I promised the girls I'd take them out for breakfast. They'll be up by eight; I'll bring you something back. Would you like waffles or pancakes?"

"Pancakes sound great. How late can I sleep?"

"Sleep as long as you like. I won't be gone longer than an hour and a half, but I'll make sure the girls are quiet until you get up."

"Thanks again Anthony. Goodnight."

"It's my pleasure Angel. Sleep tight."

Marcie took a shower and changed into the t-shirt and shorts Anthony left for her on the bed. She had barely finished her prayers when she felt her eyes getting heavy. She was asleep and resting peacefully within minutes.

Anthony made a final walk through of the condo before he turned on the alarm. Maxine and Mavis were both asleep. He repositioned them in their beds and adjusted their blankets.

He walked by the master suite and listened. Through the door he could hear Marcie snoring. It sounded like a soft whisper. Anthony smiled and headed back to the front room. He turned the television first to ESPN and then began to search for something remotely interesting. It was nearly 1 a.m. when he finally drifted off to sleep.

Chapter 5

Marcie and Anthony

Marcie was up by nine, but the condo was quiet. She brushed her teeth and got dressed. When she walked into the front room she immediately began to smile.

On the table she found a glass of orange juice and sliced fruit along with a note from Anthony.

I figured you'd be up before I returned so I left you a breakfast snack. Save room for your pancakes. We'll be back soon. Me casa is your casa. And I mean that. Kisses and Hugs. – Anthony

Marcie listened to the news as she enjoyed her fruit. As if cued, Anthony and the girls walked in the front door as she finished her glass of juice. Maxine and Mavis led the way. They raced over to Marcie to give her a hug. "Daddy wouldn't let us get you up for breakfast." Mavis sang.

Excited like her sister, "But we brought you some pancakes." Maxine added.

"You do like pancakes don't you?" Mavis asked before Marcie could respond.

"Thanks. I love pancakes." Marcie smiled.

"You guys go to your rooms and play. Once Ms. Marcie has had breakfast we'll go to the park for a bit." Anthony added with a smile.

Anthony placed Marcie's pancakes on the table in front of her along with a glass of milk. Marcie wasted no time cutting into her food. Anthony sat at the table and watched as she devoured each bite. He could tell by the look on Marcie's face that she'd gotten some rest and that made him feel accomplished.

Marcie broke the silence by thanking Anthony again for making her feel welcome. "I think I slept better last night than I have in years. Thanks for your kindness. I know you don't mind, but what I want you to understand is that I really appreciate everything you've done.

"You're welcome. It is always my pleasure to make you feel at home. I'm counting on my home being our home," He paused and then said, "one day."

Marcie smiled. "You keep spoiling me like this and you might just get lucky Mr. Monesta."

"I'm counting on that." Anthony quickly replied.

Marcie

Marcie fell back on her sofa. She was exhausted. Maxine and Mavis had spent hours running around the park. They'd played on every single piece of park equipment.

Marcie scanned the channels on the television and quickly decided there was nothing on worth missing her nap. She turned off the television and turned on her CD player. Listening to jazz was a great way to start an afternoon nap. Within minutes Marcie was dreaming.

Marcie woke to knocking on her door. She rubbed her eyes and looked over at the clock. Her afternoon nap had lasted nearly four hours.

She immediately sprang up. Anthony and the girls must have been at the door. She looked through the peep hole and just as she thought the little knocks belonged to Maxine and Mavis. Those two were like energizer bunnies. Marcie smiled and opened the door.

"Hi, munch-kins. How was your nap?"

The girls smiled and replied in unison. "We didn't take a nap. Daddy, just made us lay down. We weren't sleepy. We wanted to see you." The girls pushed by Marcie and took their place on the empty couch.

"Looks like someone did take a nap." He kissed Marcie and followed her into the apartment.

"Yeah, a long nap. I'm not ready yet. Well, I guess that's obvious. Find the girls something to watch on television. It's going to take me awhile."

"We'll be fine. I'm glad you were able to get some rest, because it's going to take both of us to keep up with those two."

Marcie smiled and headed for her bedroom. She emerged thirty minutes later wearing jeans, sneakers, a red t-shirt, and a smile.

As soon as Maxine saw Marcie she looked at Anthony and asked, "Can we leave now daddy? I'm hungry."

"Yes, Maxie, get your jacket."

Anthony helped Marcie with her jacket and within minutes they were in the car and on their way to Maxwell's. Maxwell's had become their safe haven. It was where they had their first date and in fact where Anthony first realized he wanted to spend the rest of his life making Marcie happy.

As they drove Marcie thought back to she and Anthony's first date. It seemed like years had passed since then, but in actuality, it was a little less than a year ago. She'd never expected to build a long term relationship with Anthony. She was just hoping to get through the first date without panicking. The truth was Anthony made her feel like companionship was worth the effort. Being with Anthony and the girls made her feel alive and even though she was afraid, Marcie was excited about the possibility of having a real family – experiencing real love. She hated comparing Anthony to David but David was all she knew and the more she realized Anthony was nothing like David – the more she let down her guard. She was hopeful.

Chapter 6

David

David had signed himself into a homeless shelter as Donald and enjoyed the idea of not being in prison. He had talked to a contractor working in a subdivision within walking distance of the shelter about helping out. He expected to have a job by the end of the week.

The shelter was supported by St. Peters Baptist Church which was a site for the AA Group that he was attending. David was determined to turn his life around. He had no intention of spending another day in prison.

"Hi Donald." Walter another resident in the shelter greeted him with the false name he was now using as his own.

"Hi, Walt. How's it going man?"

"Everything is looking pretty good. The guy at the end of the block has agreed to let me come in and help him clean up twice a week and a few of the other business owners said they'd consider it. Things are looking up."

"Things are good for me too. I should have something by the end of the week too. Say Walt, what are you doing tonight?"

"Well, I think I'm going to talk to a few more of the business owners. You know, hit them up before the dry cleaner smell fades from my shirt. It sure was nice of Ms. Peters to bring clothes for us to go to job interviews. Why? What do you have planned?"

"I was thinking about staying for church service after the meeting tonight thought you might want to join me."

"Not me. I'm not up for that church stuff tonight."

"Okay man. I'll catch you later." David understood how Walt felt. He enjoyed the service, but some of the people were down-right rude. If looks could kill he'd be dead, but he decided that attending church was more important than the stares of people, especially if he wanted to stay out of prison. He needed support and other than his brother Jacob, his family would not talk to him. Before he started drinking all the time he enjoyed going to church. He hoped that things would be as good now as they were then.

David walked down the street towards St. Peters - if he could only be invisible. He hated pretending not to notice that someone else was pretending to be so caught up in their conversation to speak to him as he walked by. He realized the church was made up of "faith-ers" and "fakers". There was no avoiding either group so he prepared his mind to accept whoever he encountered.

Two and a half hours later from the crowd of worshippers exiting St. Peters emerged David, with a smile on his face. He was glad he'd gone.

Chapter 7

David

A few months passed and David was determined to stay out of prison. His greatest hope was that he could find a stable job and blend in with all of the other hardworking people around him. He knew that attending AA would be essential and he had not missed a meeting in three months. So far he had managed to find a contractor willing to offer work two or three times a week. He wasn't making a lot, but he was happy to have a source of income.

He was feeling better about himself. He wasn't sure he'd ever be able to amend for his past but he sure was going to try. At the last AA meeting he'd volunteered to work with the Men's Ministry at St. Peter's in their annual back to school blast. They focused on working with the teenagers from the local high school encouraging them to stay in school and just talking to them about the pitfalls they needed to avoid. For the first time in years he felt secure and committed to accomplishing something worthwhile. As he walked back to the shelter, he looked in each shop window. He was imagining himself walking in making purchases without worrying about the cost. Then as he neared the men's clothing store, he noticed a lady standing near the curb waiting for the light to change. Even with a hooded jacket, there was something familiar about her stance. Before David could figure out what it was, the woman crossed the street and boarded the bus. David turned his attention back to the new suit hanging in the display window. When he saved up enough money, he was going to buy him a new suit and shoes. He hated going to church in jeans. David gazed into the window for a few more minutes and then continued his walk to the shelter. By the time he reached the front door, he could smell dinner. Smiling to himself, *"Tonight smelled like fried chicken and collard greens."* Ms. Peters always made special dinners for Friday night. She said it was her way of making up for residents having a curfew on a Friday night. Saturday was special too. She did everything she could think of to keep the residents on the right path. David smiled as he took in the aroma. Tonight would be a great night and today had been a great day. One step at a time he was going to make a new start. It wasn't until he went to bed that night that he remembered the woman on the corner again. It had been Marcie. He was sure of it. He was up for the rest of the night wondering how many times he'd walked past her in the months since he'd been on the run. What were the chances he'd stop in the very town she moved to? His thoughts were racing. He couldn't sleep. At four o'clock he finally convinced himself that the woman he saw was just someone who resembled Marcie. There was no way he'd chosen Marcie's new home to try and hide out. He had to have been mistaken. David closed his eyes and prayed for a peaceful rest. He knew he only had a couple of hours.

Marcie

Marcie woke up startled by the sound of...a rooster crowing? She looked around the room trying to locate the sound. Finally, she'd found it. It was the alarm on her cell phone. Anthony must have set it before he left. The sound was so obnoxious. She reached for the phone and then realized she had no idea how to turn it off. She began to push buttons and finally it stopped.

Marcie had been back at work for a couple of months, but yesterday was the first time she'd gone beyond work, church, Anthony's house and the grocery store. Anthony's birthday was in two weeks and she'd gone to a store in the neighboring town to try and find something special. Her boss had suggested Chastane's Men's Apparel because the owner took pride in having custom designs. She'd found something she liked, but had not been able to settle on the color so she decided to sleep on it and go back at the end of the week. For the first time in weeks she had enjoyed the afternoon without worrying about David. No doubt he was hundreds of miles away if he knew what was good for him. Believing that was the only thing that allowed her to sleep at night.

David

David could smell pancakes and bacon. He knew it was time for him to get up, but he felt like he had just gone to sleep. David got up slowly. He wished he could just sleep for one more hour, but he knew if he didn't get up right now he'd miss breakfast and be late for work. David spent the majority of his day thinking about how he could have made different choices and how much better his life would be if he had just refused to use alcohol and drugs. He'd no doubt be happily married to Marcie. Marcie, she was all he could think about for the last two days. Since he saw the lady on the curb, thoughts of Marcie flooded his mind. His thoughts bounced between his past with Marcie and his present predicament.

David's thoughts slowly drifted toward making the best of his life now. He had no way of knowing how long his freedom would last. As he walked towards the men's store that he passed twice each day, he decided today was the day he'd go in and try on one of those suits. Walter always talked about dreams and making them real. He decided today was the day he'd feel one of those suits against his skin and see what he'd look like once he'd saved enough money. As he neared the door, he contemplated turning back, but he was almost pulled inside by the salesperson.

"Hello sir. Can I help you find something? We have all of our latest arrivals 10% off today and we do offer layaway services."

Stunned David just smiled.

The persistent salesman continued. "Which one would you like to try on?"

David thought to himself, if he had known he would get this kind of reception, he would have come in weeks ago.

Pointing to the dark gray suit, "I'd like to try that one."

"Excellent choice..." the salesman responded. "It is perfect for your height and build."

David tried three different suits before he decided to go back to his original choice. He was admiring himself in the body length mirror outside the dressing room when he saw her standing at the check-out counter. It was Marcie. Where had she come from? He thought to himself, *"Man, she is beautiful."* He quickly ducked back into the dressing room. He sat on the bench in the dressing room. He didn't know what to do. First, he needed to change clothes. He sat on the bench in the dressing room trying to figure out what to do next. He was convinced that running into her was no coincidence. He had to know where she lived now and why she was buying men's clothing. Was she remarried? He had to know. David stood inside the dressing room door until he heard the salesman wish Marcie a good day. Then, he walked out slowly. He gave the salesman a quick, "not today" and walked out onto the street.

Marcie was standing on the curb waiting for the bus just as he had seen her days before. He pulled his cap down over his eyes and flipped the collar up on his jacket. He knew he was taking a big chance, but he couldn't resist the temptation.

David watched passenger after passenger shuffle onto the bus and at the last moment he popped on his shades and got on the bus. He noticed Marcie was halfway back talking steadily to someone on her cell phone. If he were lucky she'd be so distracted she wouldn't even look his way. If he wasn't lucky he'd be back in jail before the 11 o'clock news. Maybe this was a stupid idea after all. David contemplated getting off the bus as the doors closed and the bus moved slowly down the street. He couldn't believe he was risking getting caught.

He leaned against the window and waited for the next stop. At the next stop three more passengers got on, but no one got off. Three stops later the bus was only half full, and David was terrified that his freedom was slipping away. He regretted his impulsiveness. He realized that being impulsive was one of the reasons he ended up in prison in the first place. When it came to Marcie he just couldn't think straight. When he thought about it, she had always done right by him. She had always treated him with respect. She cared about him even though he didn't realize it at the time. He had treated her more like a doormat. Instead of protecting her, he would get drunk and abuse her. David could feel the heat rising from his neck to his cheeks. Marcie had been his first love and in the early years they were so connected that they could communicate without speaking a word, but the challenges of living a wild life had come between them. He still didn't remember all of the details of that last night they were together, but he remembered enough to know that he could burn in hell for his actions. He wished that he could tell Marcie he had changed. He wanted nothing more than to see her recover from all of the pain he'd caused her. He didn't want to see her with anyone else, but he knew she would never be with him again.

The bus stopped again. He could see that Marcie was picking up her bags. He turned and looked out the window hoping to go unnoticed. Just as Marcie approached his seat on the bus her cell phone rang. She began to dig through her bags for the phone. David was relieved.

He watched as she stepped onto the sidewalk and then he got up. Several people were between him and Marcie, but he noticed one man that looked out of place. After the time he'd spent in prison, he could spot trouble. Every time Marcie slowed down this guy would slow down as well. After a few blocks of watching Marcie's movements and looking at the man to see how he was responding, David turned his full attention to this unknown man. David was convinced this man had ill intentions toward Marcie and he wasn't going to allow him to carry out his plans. As Marcie neared a complex called Aspen Hill Apartments the unknown man began to slow down as if he expected Marcie to stop there. To David's surprise, Marcie walked through the gate.

David's suspicions were confirmed. This unknown man had been following Marcie. He either knew her or this was not the first time he'd followed her. David felt the need to protect her. He didn't know what this man's intentions were, but he was certain he could convince him to choose someone else.

David followed closely and watched as Marcie entered an apartment. He then looked back. The man had pulled a ski cap down over his face and was walking to the side of the apartment. There was a light chill in the air, but nothing that warranted either the long sleeved zippered jacket or the ski mask. David followed behind him and watched as he pulled a ladder from the bushes and laid it against the brick wall. It was getting dark out now, but surely he wasn't seeing this man do this at this hour of the day. David also noticed the man had pulled on a tool belt. He seemed to be trying to look as if he fit in, but David wasn't buying it. The ladder was near an open window. David realized the window led to Marcie's apartment when he saw the lights come on in the front room of the apartment. He moved with a new sense of urgency. He picked up a tree branch and as he approached the man who had begun to climb the ladder, he aimed for his knees. The unknown man let out a half audible groan and fell to the ground. David immediately hit him once more with the tree branch and then he snatched the cap off of his face and whispered into the man's ear. The fear that gripped the unknown man's eyes confirmed for David that he understood his message. The man slowly crawled out of David's reach and then he pulled himself upright and slowly jogged away. The severity of his encounter with David and the tree branch was evident because now the unknown man had a limp.

David regained his composure. He could feel his heart beating. He followed the unknown man until he boarded the bus and David was sure he wouldn't return.

He couldn't believe what had just happened. Realizing that someone might have seen the altercation and called the police, he dared not return to Marcie's duplex to tell her what just happened, or to warn her to be more careful of her surroundings. At least now he knew he wasn't imagining things. Maybe

God had allowed him to end up in Marcie's town so that he could save her from any further harm. He was thankful to God for allowing him to be there.

Chapter 8

Monique and Kent

It had been a few days since Monique had spoken to Marcie or Anthony so she was excited about tonight's party for Anthony. She loved playing hostess and seeing Marcie again would be great.

The evening was full of laughter and all of Anthony's favorite dishes. It was great to have the family together again.

Monique had pulled out all of the board games she could find (Scrabble, Taboo, Monopoly, chess and even checkers). Ending the night with board games had become a tradition and tonight wouldn't be an exception. Unfortunately, at the last couple of events the games had been interrupted by unexpected news.

Considering the fact that David was on the run and Marcie, as well as, the rest of the family was already on guard, Monique wasn't prepared for any new surprises. After hours of entertaining themselves, the girls began to promenade into the den. Mavis was the first to speak up. "Daddy are you gonna cut the cake?"

Marcie smiled, "That's right. What's a party without cake and ice cream?"

As if they were all waiting for their cue, they all crowded around the table and watched as Monique lit the candles.

Anthony pulled Marcie to the side. "Don't eat too much cake and ice cream. I don't want you to get sleepy. I have a birthday speech I want to share with you later and I'll need your full, undivided attention." He leaned over and placed a light kiss on Marcie's forehead and then without giving her a chance to respond, he nudged her towards the table which now had a cake glowing with candles surrounded by smiling faces and eager hands.

Marcie was intrigued by Anthony's behavior. She couldn't hide the fact that she was glowing with anticipation of his "birthday speech." She hoped no one else would notice. Anthony always knew how to get into her head and make her smile from within. She couldn't believe how amazing he made her feel. She felt secure, loved, happy - even full of joy. With Anthony there was rarely a dull moment.

"Marcie...Marcie...Marcie?" Marcie's thoughts were interrupted by someone calling her name. She turned around to see Monique and Megan who was the co-owner of Heart to Heart and the best friend of Monique, waving to her to escape with them to the kitchen. She slowly walked towards them, but she was still thinking about how wonderful her life was at this moment.

Megan spoke first. She was whispering. "Come on girl. Hurry before they realize we've left." As they entered the kitchen, Megan spoke again. "I saw Anthony pull you aside and you have been in a daze since then. Are you holding out on us? Did he pop the question?"

Marcie gasped. "Oh, Lord no. I don't know what I'd do if he did. I don't think...I mean I don't know..." Marcie stopped and just smiled. "He is a wonderful man. I just can't help but think there has to be something I'm missing. No one can be that perfect."

Megan spoke first. "You're right no one is THAT perfect, but I do believe that God will allow us to meet the "perfect - IMPERFECT" person to share this life on earth with and it looks like your "perfect - IMPERFECT" man has found you. Don't be scared Marcie. Enjoy your relationship with Anthony. I know there is a lot of uncertainty with David being out there but don't shut down. Continue to enjoy your life and know that God is watching over you. Live girl. Laugh." Megan gave Marcie a quick hug and then continued. "I better go rescue the cake and ice cream or these girls will be up all night."

As Megan walked out, Monique walked over to Marcie slowly. "You have a look on your face Marcie. What is it? Are you okay?"

"Yes, I'm fine." Marcie spoke softly. "You guys talk so confidently about God and what he can do. I wish I could do that and feel as confident as you seem about what I was saying. I've always gone to church Monique, but I don't think I have the same kind of feelings you have about God. I've heard you talk about having a relationship with God. I don't truly have that. Well, I don't feel like I do. There has to be more."

Monique was surprised by Marcie's confession and honesty; she reached out to her and spoke softly, "Marcie you can have a personal relationship with God. God wants a relationship with you. Do you mind if I share some things with you before we go back to the den?"

Marcie spoke up quickly, "Will you? I need to know."

Monique walked with Marcie into her office and pulled out a couple of bibles from the desk. She turned first to Genesis and shared the story of the creation. She then turned to John and talked about God being love, and how much he loved the world to give his own son. She made a point to let Marcie know that all had sinned and fallen short of the glory of God. Each thing she shared with Marcie, she was sure to show her the scripture and verse in the bibles so that she could read it for herself. Then finally, she talked to Marcie about the need to believe in her heart and confess with her mouth that Jesus was Lord. Tears had begun to fill Marcie's eyes. She tried to speak, but her words were caught in her throat. Monique reached for the tissues and handed Marcie a few. Then Marcie collected her thoughts and began to speak.

"Thanks Monique. I've never really had it explained to me like that. I always thought it was complicated. I mean David grew up in church, but something had to go wrong. I mean...How could he treat me like he did? We always went to church when we were married, and yet I didn't understand how he could love the Lord and treat me so badly. I just never understood." Looking down at the floor, tears in her eyes, she continued. "After listening to you, I realize that David is the one who didn't understand the love of God. I feel sorry for him now." Marcie continued softly, "But I do understand how Anthony really is a different man. He truly knows and understands the love of God and that's why he treats me so well."

Monique and Marcie's conversation was interrupted by Kent sticking his head in the door. "Hey you guys, you've been gone for over an hour, and we've eaten all of the cake and half of the ice cream."

Monique and Marcie both exploded in laughter. There was enough cake for forty people and 5 gallons of ice cream, but Kent was convincing.

Monique waved Kent away, "We'll be down in five minutes, sweetheart."

Kent smiled, blew her a kiss and disappeared down the hallway.

Monique returned her gaze to Marcie. "Marcie this is only the beginning. I want you to have this Bible and I'll work with you as much as you like to develop the personal relationship with God you desire. This is one of the bibles I use to highlight my favorite scriptures. My favorites are the ones that include promises, so if you read the highlighted parts you'll find a lot of the things that God has promised us as His children. One thing that I remind myself of often that has helped me face a lot of challenges is "I am who God says I am." No matter how bad things look, how bad I feel, what other people say about me – remember these words "I am who God says I am." Then look in the bible and find some of the things God says about you. Don't worry I promise to walk this journey with you for as long as it's necessary. Before long you'll be encouraging me. Now, let's get back before they send Anthony for us. We'll talk again soon. I promise things will get better."

"Thanks Monique. They already are." Marcie gave Monique a quick hug as they walked down the hallway towards the den.

Anthony and Marcie

"Thanks Marcie for spending the evening with me. This was the best way I could imagine celebrating turning forty - having you there, my girls and my family and you.

Marcie smiled. "You already said me."

Anthony smiled then his smiled turned serious and Marcie could feel butterflies in her stomach. Anthony sensed her nervousness and spoke quickly to relieve her concerns.

"Marcie I don't want you to ever be afraid of me. I want you to know that I will always be your protector. I want you to feel safe all the time, but even safer when I am around. You are a beautiful woman inside and out. I know you don't always feel that way, but I see it. I sense it when I'm with you. I hear it in your voice and I feel the beauty in your touch. I am certain that I want to indulge in your beauty for the rest of my life, but I won't pressure you. I want you to feel about us the way I feel about you right now and until then I'll wait."

Marcie was relieved. She was so afraid Anthony's birthday speech would be a proposal. She didn't know what she would have done. She couldn't have told him no, but there was no way she could've said yes either. Marcie's heart skipped a beat. She really did love Anthony.

"Anthony, I was scared. You know me well. I can't express in words what you mean to me right now, but someday I will be able to and I promise you I will. For now I just want to tell you thanks for seeing beauty in me." Marcie paused then continued. "This is kinda' like a change of subject but it's really important."

Anthony focused his gaze on Marcie and encouraged her to go on.

"Anthony, Monique and I talked tonight and it's something I think you should know."

Now, for the first time Anthony was nervous. What was Marcie about to reveal? Anthony continued to listen without changing his facial expression. As Marcie continued her voice began to lower and Anthony reached for her to offer her assurance. "What is it Marcie? What is it?"

"Anthony, I think I know why things have been so hard for me. I've listened to you, Monique and Megan...Kent and Bryan. You all have a personal relationship with God. I can tell by the way you act. You all seem so loving and at the same time fearless. You are forgiving and strong even when you are hurting. I want that for my life and tonight I talked to Monique about it and she helped me begin the journey. I'd like for you to share in that journey with me. Anthony, will you pray with me? I want to be fearless, strong, forgiving and full of joy like you. Will you pray with me?"

Marcie's request the second time pulled Anthony out of his gaze. Tears had filled his eyes as he listened to Marcie speak. He could no longer hold them back. He kneeled in front of Marcie on the floor, took her hands in his and began to pray.

Anthony

Anthony woke the next morning with a smile on his face. He hadn't remembered anything about his drive home from Marcie's apartment except the fact that he praised God all the way home. This was his best birthday since Rachel died. He couldn't believe that after suffering so much loss he could experience so much joy at one time. He quietly thanked God for confirming that Marcie truly was a part of the plan for his life.

Just as suddenly as he awakened with joy the quietness of his condo made him uneasy. There should have been a lot of giggling. Then, he remembered. Monique had kept the girls. He could sleep in because eating breakfast was the last thing on his mind. God truly was a faithful God.

Chapter 9

David and Marcie

Marcie raced to the door. Anthony was early, but she was ready. She had been waiting for this date all week. She stopped a moment to check one last time in the mirror and then quickly opened the door with her arms opened wide and a smile on her face. "Hey babe, I'm...."

She stopped in mid-sentence. Her words were extinguished by fear. Her arms fell slowly to her side. She tried to run, but her legs wouldn't move. Without acknowledging her surprise, David smiled at Marcie and began to say the words he'd longed to say for months. "I'm truly sorry Marcie. I am sorry for all of the pain I caused you. I know that you may never forgive me, but I wanted you to hear it from me. I allowed the drugs and alcohol to rule me. I hated myself and I took it out on you. You are a beautiful woman and I am glad that you have found someone to love you. I only wish that it could have been me."

David finally took a breath. He realized Marcie had not moved or said a word since he had first spoken. He looked closely at her face and realized tears had formed in the corners of her eyes and then he noticed the puddle of what appeared to be water at her feet. He wasn't sure what he had expected from Marcie. He thought she might throw a lamp at him, but he had not expected this.

His thoughts were interrupted by the sound of a car door. He looked across the parking lot and saw the man he'd watched Marcie kiss goodnight at the door a few nights before. He was carrying a bouquet of roses. He looked back at Marcie. He hated to leave her like this, but he had to go or things would get really bad fast. "Marcie I just want you to know that I'm sorry. I won't ever hurt you again." He quickly turned and walked in the opposite direction away from the man approaching Marcie's door.

David's brisk walk quickly turned into a jog. He was afraid the man would be coming after him. He didn't stop until he got to the bus station. Twenty minutes later he was sitting on the back seat fuming. How could he have allowed things to get to this point? He had screwed up his and Marcie's lives. Marcie was such a strong intelligent woman when he first met her. Now, because of the things he'd done she was broken. Before now he'd seen Marcie fearless, but he realized that he'd killed that part of her. For the first time since his relationship with Marcie began, David understood the man he was and the woman Marcie had become. Failing to control his anger had destroyed his and Marcie's lives. If he could make it all right again, if he could convince Marcie he'd never hurt her again, he could live. He thought about the mess he had to deal with as he stared out of the window. He had not considered the consequences of going to Marcie's apartment again carefully enough. This time she'd surely call the police. He couldn't go back to the shelter. The cops would be looking for him. No one would believe that him ending up in the same city as Marcie was fate.

Marcie and Anthony

Anthony realizing a man was walking away from Marcie's open door quickened his steps. He was startled by Marcie standing in the doorway with tears running down her cheeks. He reached out to her and she jumped. He spoke her name softly. "Marcie, baby what's wrong? What just happened? Are you ok?"

Marcie nodded. Anthony was relieved, but confused. He could see the fear in her eyes. Something he never wanted to see again.

"Who was that?" Anthony asked. This time holding Marcie's hands in his hands encouraging her to speak.

"David. It was David." Marcie trembled as she spoke.

Anthony dropped her hands and stepped back out the door. He looked both ways but the man was nowhere in sight. He came back to Marcie. This time he noticed the puddle. "Marcie, you can't stay here tonight. Let's go get you a change of clothes." Inside Anthony was about to explode. David had some nerve following Marcie to terrorize her. The Lord only knows what would have happened if he had not arrived early. He struggled to keep his tone calm and even. "Marcie would you like to get dressed now." It was the only way he could think of to call attention to the fact that Marcie had soiled her clothes without being direct.

Marcie nodded again without saying a word. Anthony put his arm around her waist and led her to the bathroom and placed her on the bench beside the tub. He started a bubble bath. Then he walked to the bedroom to get her some clothes and to call the police. He needed to report this. David was wanted. He hoped the police could catch him this time. He whispered a prayer for strength and wisdom. He wasn't sure how to comfort Marcie. When he returned to the bathroom Marcie was in her bath with the curtain pulled. "Marcie I'm placing your clothes on the counter. I'm going to go and finish packing your overnight bag."

Determined, Marcie said, "I'm not going to run this time Anthony. I can't run all my life. I'm staying here tonight."

Anthony could tell by Marcie's tone that he wasn't going to change her mind without a fight. He was proud of her for showing strength and decided his role should be to encourage and support her not dictate to her.

"Ok sweetheart. I'll go fix you some tea. We can..."

Marcie interrupted him. "Anthony I'd still like to go out if you don't mind. I've been looking forward to this night and I'd like for us to keep our plans."

Anthony didn't know what to say. Marcie's words caught him off guard. "Ok, but if you are staying here tonight you can expect a house guest."

"Thanks. I appreciate that. I'll be out in ten minutes."

Anthony walked back to Marcie's room and unpacked her overnight bag. Then, he called Monique to see if she and Kent could keep the girls for the night. He explained David's appearance at Marcie's apartment and Marcie's unwillingness to leave. Monique agreed without hesitation. Anthony promised to call if he heard anything about David's whereabouts.

David

David paced the floor. He'd decided going back to the shelter really was his only option. Now, he had to figure out what next. He still had his job and the money he'd saved. He would stay away from Marcie's neighborhood and hope that no one came looking for him. He'd leave town as soon as he could. Then, just as quickly as he thought up that idea, he changed his mind. Who was he kidding? He couldn't stay. He rushed from corner to corner of the room gathering things he didn't want to leave behind. He'd be leaving the only real home he'd known as a sober adult. He was terrified of what his departure could mean. He had to find a place where he could worship God and stay sober.

David took a final look around the room and walked out the door. He boarded the bus on the corner and found a seat by the window. He wasn't sure where he'd end up, but he hoped, he prayed that God would have mercy on him.

Chapter 10

Marcie

Marcie lay awake in her bed listening to the silence. Knowing Anthony was in the other room was a comfort; however, not knowing if David was outside waiting to confront her again made her feel uneasy.

She lay still remembering how he'd always promise to never hurt her again, but he'd always manage to get drunk and "go off" on her. She had to admit that this time he seemed different. What was she thinking...this was the man who'd nearly ended her life, but yet there was something different about David. She couldn't explain it. Anthony would never understand, but she wished that David could have a happy life – far away from her.

Marcie hoped she'd never feel the fear she felt earlier that day when she stood face to face with David. If she learned one thing, fear wasn't of God. Fear caused her to stand paralyzed in position to be a victim once again. God willing she would never allow her fear of David to overtake her again. Marcie lay still praying to God, tears running down from the corners of her eyes and finally stopping at the edge of her hair line behind her ears.

She was certain of God's ability and willingness to meet all of her needs. She'd made it this far and she knew that was only God working in her life. She needed to be safe from David and she resolved to rely on God to keep her safe no matter what.

Marcie had almost fallen asleep again when she heard a knock on her door. "Marcie, are you okay?"

Marcie searched for the strength to speak out loud without revealing the fact that she had been crying. "I'm fine Anthony. I was just having a little trouble sleeping."

"Well, I'm up now. How about some pancakes? I feel like cooking."

Marcie smiled, "That sounds great. I'll be dressed in a few minutes."

Marcie welcomed the distraction. She'd fully expected to wake up and cry for another hour. It was nice having Anthony there. He always showed silent strength and offered comfort. He always knew exactly what to say and do. She was glad he'd decided to spend the night. She hadn't realized how terrified she was of the idea of David returning until she tried to close her eyes and go to sleep.

When Marcie entered in the kitchen twenty minutes later, Anthony was removing the bacon from the grill and flipping two plate sized pancakes. She saw the eggs and shredded cheese in the bowl on the counter. Suddenly hungry, she could hardly wait to eat. Marcie walked to the cabinet and got glasses for their milk and juice.

Today was the beginning of a new life for Marcie. She was committed to living a life of peace. She wasn't sure how because she knew David was still free, but she'd decided to trust God with her life. Anthony carefully placed her plate on the table in front of her. Marcie felt a smile come over her face. She was taken in by the concern in Anthony's eyes and instantly she was assured that her life of peace would include the man that stood before her.

Chapter 11

David

The bus stopped in front of what appeared to be a drug store. Thirteen hours on a bus was all he could take, David decided this would be his stop. He wasn't sure what to expect, but this town seemed to meet his requirements. It was small enough for him to walk to the majority of places he needed to get to and large enough for him to blend in without attracting undo attention. He'd read about this town Oxford, Mississippi. It was at the top of the list of cities to retire and raise a family. It was a college town so if he dressed right he might not be noticed for a while. He could probably work doing odd jobs.

David walked off the bus and began to check out his surroundings. He immediately spotted a wing shop across the street. Realizing he hadn't eaten anything for almost twenty-four hours, chicken sounded great. David ran through traffic across the narrow street. It was twelve forty-five and one of the busiest times of the day. College commuters, day care vans and delivery trucks filled the lanes on each of the neighboring streets. He even noticed a couple of taxies. Startled by the sound of a police siren David walked into the wing shop looking back to see where the police were. As the car passed the window David sat down in a booth and exhaled. He had to relax. He was wanted, but as long as he stayed out of trouble no one would come looking for him...at least he hoped not.

Fifteen minutes later David anticipated the arrival of his wings and he was not disappointed. After throwing back a 12pc wing meal David began to once again take in his surroundings. For the first time he noticed the help wanted sign on the bulletin board. Knowing that finding a job was one of the first things he needed to do David walked over to get a closer look.

Help Wanted: Danielle's Bed and Breakfast. Grounds keeper/Maintenance Worker. Free room plus wages. Call 662-953-7777 ask for Mrs. Mercy.

David's eyes lit up. This was an answer to his prayers. He could do this. He'd have a place to stay. Only God could have made this possible. He remembered his prayer before leaving the shelter. He wouldn't waste time calling. David quickly copied the number, then realizing he didn't have a cell phone he sat back down in the booth, lowered his head and whispered another prayer. As David opened his eyes, he noticed the pay phone on the wall in the corner. He couldn't believe it. He had definitely gotten off the bus in the "twilight zone". He laughed when he read the sign above it. *"Not just for decoration – I take dimes, nickels, and quarters."* He paused for a minute. Was God really answering his prayer? Even though he believed, he felt he wasn't worthy. Had God really forgiven him? His eyes filled with tears, but he refused to let them fall. He walked outside to get some air.

David confidently walked back inside, picked up the phone and began dialing the number. The voice on the other end seemed pleasant.

"Hello."

David swallowed before he spoke.

"Hello my name is David. I'm calling about the groundskeeper position you have been advertising. Has the position been filled?"

"Well, no it hasn't, as a matter of fact. I've had those signs up for three weeks now and you're the first to call. I was starting to think someone had pulled them all down."

David breathed a sigh of relief.

"When can you come by David? I don't do telephone interviews. I need to meet any prospective employees. Applications and background checks only reveal the known. I pride myself in being able to discern the unknown facts."

David inhaled. Then, he began to speak slowly hoping that the right words would emerge. "Well...I could stop by this afternoon or early in the morning. I don't have anything planned."

"Later this afternoon would be perfect. I have a couple that will be arriving around five thirty and I've scheduled my dinner time around them. Can you be here at six fifteen? The house is on the street right off the square - 211 Magnolia Drive. It's a white house with a wrap-around porch."

"Yes ma'am." David smiled as he replied. "I will be there." As he put the phone back on the receiver he exhaled. He couldn't give Ms. Mercy his real last name. If she did a background check, she'd certainly find out he was wanted. He had not even thought that far ahead. He had a few hours to figure out what his new last name would be. Either that or walk away, but this was too great of an opportunity to pass up. Jobs in this economy for a wanted man were extremely hard to come by. He had to take a chance.

It was 6:10 p.m. David slowly raised his hand to knock on the door in front of him. The door flew open and a grey haired man greeted him. The man extended his hand to David and spoke with a deep voice. "Good evening, I am Grayson Mercy. You must be David."

David shook his hand and offered a smile. He thought to himself. "Did he just say he was grace and mercy...God really did have a sense of humor."

The man led David into what appeared to be a formal sitting room. He motioned for David to have a seat. "I'll go get Grace. You help yourself to the iced tea. We'll join you in a few minutes."

David smiled. This was truly unbelievable. He poured himself a glass of iced tea and sat down on the nearest chair. He still had not settled on a new last name when the couple appeared.

Mrs. Mercy greeted David as if she were a long lost son. "Hello, David. You met my husband Grayson already. I am delighted you could join us. Why don't you grab your tea and join us in the dining room. Dinner is on the table. We can talk over things in there."

So far...so good, David thought. He decided that he'd just go with the flow. The Mercys seemed to be nice people.

Unless they were psychic they wouldn't know he was wanted unless he told them. He had no plans of doing that.

An hour had passed and David managed to answer all of the questions without telling a lie. He was both surprised and pleased. Then like a marksman Grace Mercy launched her next question.

"David I hope you don't think I'm being direct, but I would like to know why you got divorced."

David couldn't hide the panic that had overtaken him. He thought to himself. 'Yes you are being too direct.'- but he heard a sound that seemed to be coming from his mouth answering Grace.

"I got married young. I made a lot of unforgivable mistakes and to be honest at the time of my divorce I didn't realize I needed to be forgiven. I grew up without a lot of adult supervision and I decided early that drugs and alcohol were all I needed to get me through the day. I lost focus Mrs. Mercy, but I am determined to never make that kind of mistake again. I'm working on me. I've come to realize that Marcie...that's my ex-wife...she wasn't the problem. I was. I allowed our chances of having a successful marriage to be overshadowed by drugs and alcohol."

Grayson not Grace was the first to speak up. "It sounds like you are on the right path David. My wife is often too direct." He smiled at Grace as he continued. "But that usually doesn't stop her and she's usually a good judge of character. For some reason she likes you so we would love to offer you the job if you want it. We both understand the value of having a second chance."

David was relieved. He was sure that his last confession would cause the Mercys to turn him away. "Yes Mr. Mercy. I would love the job."

"Good. Grace, I'm going to take David around to his quarters and we'll talk a little about his duties. We'll be back shortly for desert."

Grace smiled and nodded. Grayson gave her a kiss on the cheek and led David to the small house in the back. "Grace makes the best apple cobbler. We won't spend too much time out here, because I saw the new tub of ice cream she bought yesterday. I can hardly wait, but I did want to talk to you alone for a few minutes."

Grayson paused and then began to speak again with a slower and more deliberate speech pattern. "I understand where you are in life. We all reach a crossroads. I'm not asking you to tell me anymore than you're ready to share, but I do want you to know that both me and my wife are aware that you have things in your past that you don't want to talk about. We know that this job would likely suit someone either trying to run from their past or recover from it. We believe that whether you run or recover is a choice. If you would like to recover we are more than willing to support you. If you decide to run, let us know so we can get out of the way." Grayson smiled and then his countenance took on a serious gaze. "I love my wife. She's my greatest treasure. Respect her and we'll get along fine."

David returned Grayson's gaze with one of his own. "Yes sir. I will and thank you for the job."

Grayson pointed to the front door of the small house. "Here's the key. You can go look around and tell me if you see anything missing. Grace came out as soon as you two got off the phone and restocked a few things. Don't stay too long because I can't promise you I'll be able to resist Grace's cobbler for more than a few minutes."

Grayson turned and walked back into the house. David looked from side to side taking in what would be his new home...for as long as it lasted.

For the very first time, David felt free. He realized that telling the truth was truly liberating. Today was the first time he'd actually admitted to someone besides Marcie and his counselor that his alcohol and drug usage was the cause of their problems and divorce. He'd always known, but never admitted it. Having someone hear him out and then still be willing to accept him was comforting.

David opened the door and slowly walked in. It was much nicer than he expected. Even though the furniture was old, it was well kept. The bathroom was complete with tissue, soap, shampoo...Grace had even put toothpaste and deodorant on the counter. David was speechless. He thought back to the first sermon he heard at St. Peters Baptist Church. He remembered the preacher talking about restoration. He said, "Restoration is His promise. Perspective is the key." He definitely felt like God was restoring him. David took another quick look around. Then, he headed for the kitchen and Grace's apple cobbler.

Chapter 12

David

Getting to know Grayson had been a great experience for David. He hadn't bonded with his father and Grayson seemed to be a great man to be around. He always seemed to know exactly what David was thinking. He seemed willing and ready to offer words of wisdom in daily doses. He really was making a difference in the way David viewed life. As David carried wood in for the fireplace upstairs, he couldn't help but think about how Grayson seemed to dote over him. He felt more like a wayward son trying to come back home than an employee. For the last month Grace and Grayson had become like parents to him. They ate breakfast, lunch and dinner together. They worked around the house together and even worshipped together. He felt like he had a second chance at knowing what a real family was like. One of the first things David had done in the church was become a part of the boy's mentoring program. He was living out his plan to make a difference in the lives of the young men he came into contact with. Almost the same way that Grayson was making a difference in his life. He felt like his past was being erased. He knew that someday he might have to answer for his actions, but he just hoped it wouldn't be anytime soon.

When they had visitors the Mercys simply introduced him as "Our David". David felt like he had found a new home away from all of the chaos that was his real life. He knew that he'd likely have to move on, but he hoped to enjoy the idea of being a part of a family for as long as he could.

David's thoughts were interrupted by a shout from the kitchen. It was Grace. From the tone of her voice, she was likely calling him to taste one of her latest dishes. This was one of the duties he was assigned that he happily shared with Grayson.

David placed the last of the firewood onto the stack and headed for the kitchen. He stopped dead in his tracks when he entered the door. He was shocked to see that Grace wasn't alone. Grace pretended not to notice his surprise.

"Come on David. Grayson went to the store. It's your turn to taste tonight's desert. Besides you didn't have lunch. This should hold you until dinner. Kate this is our David. David, meet Katherine Shore."

David smiled and walked into the kitchen. "Tonight we're having key lime cake David. I found this recipe on Facebook. It's really rich." When Grace mentioned she had found a recipe on Facebook, David couldn't help but grin. Many older people were afraid to use technology, especially Facebook. But the Mercys were different, in fact between them they had two iPhones, an iPad and internet subscriptions to several newspapers and magazines. Facebook was a way they stayed connected to their family and friends who lived in other parts of the country.

David picked up the fork and scooped up a piece of cake. It was so moist and sweet. Grace had really done it this time. The presence of Katherine caused him to just give Grace 'two thumbs up' instead of his usual victory dance. David sat quietly and finished his desert. The first thing he noticed was how beautiful Katherine was. He listened as she talked to Grace about her new job. Apparently, she was in the middle of relocating and staying next door with her aunt and uncle until she got settled. David couldn't remember the last time he had sat listening to beautiful women talk. In fact, he didn't remember Marcie ever having her friends over. He couldn't blame her considering he was usually drunk, high or both. For a few minutes he just sat and marveled at how women were so different from men. Listening to them talk had a soothing effect on David. He decided that being around the right woman could be therapeutic. David cleared his plate and headed for the back door.

"Thanks Grace. That was wonderful as usual. I'm going to bring in more fire wood - nice to meet you Katherine."

Grace nodded, but Katherine couldn't let this handsome hunk walk out without saying something. "Good afternoon David. It nice meeting you too. Hopefully, I'll see you 'around'."

David smiled and walked out slowly. If he didn't know better he would have thought Katherine was flirting with him, but surely she wasn't – not with Grace sitting right there. Even so, he felt nervous excitement. Katherine was a beautiful woman. He was looking forward to seeing her again.

Chapter 13

David and Katherine

David sat on the steps watching the neighbor's house. He was waiting for Katherine to get home from work. The Mercys had gone with Mrs. Shore to the hospital. David stayed behind to give Katherine the news. She'd left her cell phone at home that day and her aunt hadn't been able to reach her.

Mr. Shore had fallen off the roof earlier and fractured his hip. Because of his age, his doctors were monitoring him closely before beginning surgery. David's job was to tell Katherine the news and keep her company. Mr. Shore had been taken to Memphis for the procedure and it was too late to drive that distance.

As Katherine turned into the driveway she noticed David sitting on the steps next door. He was looking especially handsome today with his fitted jeans and ribbed shirt. She couldn't believe she'd been staying with her aunt and uncle for almost six months and had only seen David twice. The Mercys sure kept him busy.

David was apprehensive as he watched Katherine get out of her car. His legs should have been moving, but he felt as if he had been glued to the step. She was so beautiful and now he was going to have to give her the bad news and ruin her day.

If only she didn't look so happy, but she did.

David knew he should have called out to her as she excited her car, but the only thing he could do was smile and wave back. He thought about how wonderful it would be to capture this moment. Then, he realized – Katherine had walked into the house without him talking to her.

Katherine put her keys on the hook in the foyer. The house was unusually quiet and there were no smells coming from the kitchen. That was odd. She quickly thought back to David sitting on the porch. If only she had been courageous enough to go over and speak to him. Then, she reminded herself "it's his job to pursue". If he is interested he should come over and talk to me.

Just as she finished her thought, she heard the doorbell ring. Startled she turned and looked towards the door. She realized there was absolutely no noise in the house. Walking to the door, she decided she must be home alone.

When she looked through the front window and saw David standing on the front porch all she could do was smile. As she opened the door, Katherine tried to appear relaxed, but the butterflies in her stomach were evidence that she was far from relaxed.

As the door opened David searched for words. He couldn't believe it. He was nervous. "Hi Katherine, I'm your neighbor."

"Hi David, I remember you."

"I came over to tell you that your aunt and uncle are with the Mercys."

"Oh ok – I thought the house was quiet and when I didn't smell dinner I knew something wasn't right. Where did they go?"

"Well, everyone is going to be ok?"

"Ok!" David could see the panic in Katherine's eyes. That was exactly what he was trying to avoid.

"Yes. Katherine everyone and everything will be fine. Do you mind stepping outside for a minute and having a seat?"

"Yes I mind. What's going on?"

David could tell she wasn't going to make it easy so he was going to just tell her and hope for the best.

"This morning Mr. Shore fell off the roof."

"The roof - what in the world was he doing on the roof? Where is he? I have to go."

"He is in Memphis. He's in critical care, but he's going to be fine. Your aunt said that you should wait until tomorrow morning to come and I will go with you."

"I'm going tonight."

"No, you are not. It's too far for you to drive alone at night."

"I thought you said you were going with me."

"I am but we should wait until in the morning."

David could tell from the look on her face that the water works were about to begin and he wasn't prepared for that. Through tears Katherine began to rant. "I can't believe I left my stupid phone at home today of all days. Aunt Jane must be going crazy with worry. Why was my Uncle James on that roof anyway? What was he thinking?"

She looked at David as if she wanted answers. He wasn't sure how to respond. He decided to avoid the emotions all together. "Have you eaten dinner Katherine?"

Katherine looked confused. "No".

"Well, how about I cook us dinner while you call and check on Mr. Shore?"

Now Katherine looked frustrated. "Okay."

"I'm going to go and get dinner started. You stay here and do what you usually do to relax after work and I'll have your dinner ready in forty-five minutes. Oh yeah, one more thing. May I have your car keys, please? Your Aunt Jane warned me that you were head-strong and hard-headed like your Uncle James."

Katherine rolled her eyes at David and pointed to the keys on the hook in the foyer. Let him take the keys. She didn't care. She had a spare set and she wasn't hard-headed either.

David grabbed the keys and headed back across the street. "You can come over as soon as you like. I'll leave the side door unlocked."

Katherine was annoyed with David and not sure if she wanted to eat his meal. "Whatever."

David smiled inside as he walked off the porch. I guess I hit a nerve. He was glad Mrs. Shore had remembered Katherine had a spare set of keys and moved them. Otherwise, he probably would be chasing taillights. "Forty five minutes tops."

Katherine couldn't believe he had spoken to her like that. He acted as if he knew her. She caught herself ranting even in her own thoughts. This man had just offered to prepare dinner for her. That wasn't something that happened every day. In fact, she hadn't eaten dinner with a handsome man in months and she couldn't remember anyone as handsome as David. Katherine's thoughts were interrupted by the ring of the phone.

"Hello. Hi, Aunt Jane. How's Uncle James? ...Yes ma'am...He just left...Yes ma'am...I understand. I'll see you in the morning."

After hanging up with her Aunt Jane, Katherine went upstairs to change into a pair of jeans and a t-shirt. She was glad to hear that her Uncle James was talking and joking with the staff. Her aunt had also instructed her to be nice to David because he was a "nice young man." Obviously, David had all of the women "eating out of the palm of his hand." Her aunt seemed to like him as much as Mrs. Mercy did. Katherine respected her Aunt Jane's opinion so she'd try to be nice to him, but he had better not call her hard-headed again. She smiled. Why did that bother her so much? After all, she knew she was stubborn. If her aunt had not called, she would have been searching for her spare key and on her way to Memphis.

Chapter 14

David and Katherine

The night before had been quite nice. David had grilled a couple of steaks along with baked potatoes and a tossed salad. After dinner they talked for hours about how they grew up and how they ended up here. Now as they rode along the interstate towards Memphis it seemed like there was nothing more to talk about. There was an awkward silence.

After several minutes, David broke the silence. "Does your radio work?"

"Yes, I'm sure it does. I rarely listen to it though."

"May I find a station?"

"Sure."

Katherine was happy that David broke the silence, but disappointed by his station. She found the majority of the topics on the radio talk shows annoying and this morning's episode was no exception. After several minutes, she decided it would be less painful if they just talked about something – anything.

"David, did you participate in sports in high school?"

"Yes. I played basketball and football for a couple of years. By the time, I was a junior I decided that organized sports required time that I didn't have to sacrifice. I had to work to help my mom pay the bills. Looking back, I probably could have done both. I had several friends who worked and participated in sports. But the truth is I probably wouldn't have gotten my HS diploma if I had tried to do that. I wasn't disciplined enough."

"I can't imagine you not being disciplined."

"I've changed a lot over the years. Fortunately, you didn't have the pleasure of meeting that David. I still struggle, but I'm definitely not the man I used to be."

"I don't think any of us are -what we used to be. God has a way of changing us. Despite popular belief, I'm not as stubborn as I used to be." Katherine smiled.

David couldn't help, but laugh out loud, "Really now!"

They continued to talk about high school and how they grew up. Before they realized it, they were in Memphis and it was time to focus on finding the hospital.

"I put the address into the GPS last night before I went to bed, but I'll need you to help if you don't mind. I can get lost in a match box. "

Surprised David reached for the device. "You really are always prepared."

"No not really, but I've gotten lost enough times to never travel without a good back up plan."

"Well according to these directions we are only a couple of miles away. You'll turn right on Canal Street and the hospital is one mile down on the left."

Katherine was focused on the traffic. It was eight o'clock and the traffic was heavy. Katherine hated driving in city traffic. She hoped David would just be quiet until they arrived at the hospital.

It took nearly twenty minutes for them to travel the two miles to the hospital. It seemed as if they were caught by every light. To Katherine's delight David remained silent. It was as if he read her mind.

Once they pulled into the hospital parking lot Katherine broke the silence. "I hate driving in traffic. I'm glad that's over."

David smiled. "You did just fine. I don't like heavy traffic either."

David grabbed the overnight bag that Mrs. Mercy asked him to bring. As they walked down the hallway to the critical care unit, David thought about how he'd enjoyed spending time with Katherine.

"Katherine, I just wanted to let you know that you are good company. I know that this wasn't under ideal circumstances, but I've enjoyed talking to you."

"I have enjoyed spending time with you too David – even if you did call me hard-headed."

David was about to protest, but then noticed the smirk on Katherine's face. She was ribbing him.

Chapter 14

Jane and James Shore

Katherine and David

Katherine noticed how tired her aunt Jane looked. She must have been up all night, she thought to herself. She immediately gave her a hug. "How's Uncle James?"

"He's fine. The doctor said the surgery will take several hours. They took him in at six-thirty so I expect someone to come out soon and give us an update."

"Ok. Have you eaten breakfast?" Katherine asked.

"No, I'm not hungry," replied Mrs. Shore.

"Well, you still need to eat something. David and I will find the cafeteria and get you a breakfast sandwich."

Katherine walking towards David, "Do you mind helping me find the cafeteria?"

"No, I don't mind. I'd like something to drink." David added.

Once Katherine and David reached the cafeteria they ordered breakfast and took a seat. David could tell Katherine was worried.

"Your Uncle James is a strong man. He'll be okay. He'll recover quickly."

"I'm not as worried about him as I am Aunt Jane. She really looks tired and that's just not good for her health. I know she's worried about Uncle James, but she CANNOT eat like this! She has to take care of her own health, or she and Uncle James will need someone to take care of them both. Emotionally Katherine continued, "Let's hurry and get back so Aunt Jane can eat."

"I hate to see you worried like this, but I do understand why you are upset." David wanted to reassure her. "All you can do is offer help. She loves your uncle and she probably doesn't have an appetite." Taking a bite of the sandwich, he continued, "At least the sandwiches are good. Don't worry. Your support will make a difference. They will both be fine. I'll do what I can to help you see to that. The Shores are good people."

"Thanks David. I appreciate your understanding and your encouraging words. Let's start by force feeding Aunt Jane this sandwich if we have too." For the first time since they arrived Katherine smiled and David could feel his heart melt. He'd done that. He'd made her smile and he was proud of that. He'd caused pain for so long it felt good to make a woman smile.

When Katherine and David returned Uncle James was out of surgery and in recovery. The doctors reported that the surgery went well and Uncle James was expected to make a complete recovery. Aunt Jane could eat now. Her mood was lighter and she even smiled as she thanked everyone for their support.

Grace and Grayson had spent the majority of the morning in the chapel praying. They offered thanks to God for answered prayer upon hearing the news about James.

Chapter 15

Katherine and David

In the weeks that followed Uncle James' surgery, Aunt Jane spent as much time as she could with him at the rehabilitation facility. Katherine was left at home alone quite often. She spent a great deal of time with David. They soon became good friends. After several evenings of dinner, movies, long walks, and staying up half the night talking, David felt as if Katherine was trustworthy. She was certainly compassionate and he needed to talk to someone. He needed to clear his head. His secrets were eating him up inside especially since he had rededicated his life to Christ. He felt the need to confess to someone.

One night after dinner while they walked under the light of the moon, David decided to open up to Katherine. He began by telling Katherine how much he enjoyed spending time with her and how important her friendship was to him.

"Katherine we've talked a lot about our childhood, but not much about our lives as adults. I'd like to tell you something that I've been thinking a lot about. I haven't shared it with anyone since I moved here."

Katherine could tell David was serious, but she couldn't help making a joke. "Oh no, are we telling secrets now? I'm not sure I'm ready for such a commitment."

David smiled. "So now you're afraid of commitment?"

Katherine tensed slightly, "Go ahead tell me your story. Should we pinky swear first?"

David held out his pinky and they went through the motions. He figured Katherine wasn't going to say anything serious but he knew she'd listen so he began by telling her that he was a recovering alcohol and drug addict. He was surprised by her response.

"I can tell by your skin and you also look a little older than you say you are. All of the people in my family who either drink a lot or have used drugs for any period of time look older than they really are. I'm not surprised by that. Is that your big secret?"

"No, it's not. That habit got me into a lot of trouble and led to some things that I am ashamed of."

"We all have a past David. Every one of us has a past."

"I know, but not everyone's past is as colorful as mine. You ready for the next part."

"Sure, your secrets are easy."

David paused for a minute and then he spoke slowly and deliberately. "Promise you won't run."

"Run. David don't be silly. Tell me the secret already."

"I have spent several years in prison. In fact, I've been out less than a year."

Katherine didn't speak for almost a full minute, but she didn't run. "Well, I guess you do have real secrets. You have my attention now. What happened?"

"Well, without going into all the details." David felt himself choking up. It was hard for him to talk about what he'd done to Marcie. "I assaulted someone in my family. I almost killed that person. I deserved to go to prison, but I've changed. I wanted to talk to someone about it, because I need to know how I can prove to them that I'm not that man anymore."

Katherine was surprised by David's confession, but she did everything she could to conceal her surprise. She realized it must have been hard for David to trust her and even though her first thought was to get away from David as fast as she could, she knew she couldn't turn her back on him.

"David, I honestly don't know what to tell you to do besides praying. I don't imagine you have an open communication with that family member. Well, I know I'd find it difficult to believe you had changed if it were me. I guess I should just share my secret and then you'll understand what I mean." Katherine paused and then continued. "No one knows this besides a couple of my former co-workers. I quit my job and moved here because I was trying to get away from an abusive boyfriend."

"Justin was verbally, physically and emotionally abusive. He cheated and then acted as if I had no right to be angry or ask him questions. I remember the night I knew I had to get away. I was supposed to meet him for dinner at 7 pm at his place: however, I got off work early and arrived at 6:15 pm. He loved deserts so I had stopped and picked up a couple of slices of our favorite caramel cake. We'd been dating for 3 and half years and I had a key to his place. When I entered the apartment, I immediately noticed a pair of red pumps on the couch and a matching purse. I heard what sounded like music playing and then I heard voices. I realized Justin wasn't alone and that this wasn't going to be a good experience. I debated what to do next. I finally had proof that he was cheating, but before I could come up with a plan Justin walked into the living room. His eyes stretched wide with surprise. He was followed closely by a girl who looked like she couldn't be more than twenty-one. She was buttoning up her blouse. When she saw me she buttoned the last few buttons quickly and reached quickly for her shoes and purse. She looked at Justin, leaned forward and gave him a kiss. Then, the next words she spoke chilled me to the bone. 'I'll see you next week sweetie. It was nice to finally meet you Katherine.' She actually knew who I was. I was in shock. The closing of the door snapped me back to reality. Instead of speaking, I glared at Justin as if my look would pierce a hole in his skin. I turned to walk away, but I was jerked backwards and slammed against the wall before I realized it. He asked me where I thought I was going. I could tell by the look on his face that this was not going to end well. He was furious. He grabbed me by the throat with one hand and pressed against me with his chest. I could smell the alcohol on his breath. He was always unreasonable when he was drinking. I was the one that should have been angry, but he always seemed to turn things around on me and that night was nothing different. He pushed me to the bedroom with his hand still around my throat and then he pushed me on the bed." Katherine paused for a moment. She had to remind herself that she was safe now.

David pulled her close hoping to reassure her. At the same time he was thinking about the pain he had caused Marcie. He could see it in Katherine's eyes. She had been terrified.

Katherine continued. Tears were now rolling down her cheeks. "He raped me David and then told me I belonged to him. He wouldn't let me leave for three days. Finally, when I convinced him I'd be back that afternoon after I attended my monthly staff meeting, he let me go. I didn't know what to do so I went to my apartment and packed as many clothes as I could in my luggage and didn't turn back. I didn't know what to do or where to go."

"I actually hid out with a couple of friends and in a few hotels for a month before I was able to find a new job and get the nerve to ask my aunt and uncle if I could stay with them. I didn't tell them about Justin. I just talked about my new job and how wonderful it would be to live close to my family. I've always been one of their favorites. When my parents died they took over as my counselors. They really are more than an aunt and uncle to me. I'm still healing David. Betrayal, coupled with physical abuse changes a person. I don't know if that person will ever forgive you. Only God can bring that change about. I've been praying for months now. I know I need to forgive Justin, but I have no desire to forgive him. Yet, I have no choice but to depend on God to bring about that change in me. I think that if you want your family member to forgive you, you will have to depend on God too."

"Katherine, I'm sorry to unload my burdens on you. I didn't mean to bring up bad memories for you. I'm sorry that you were hurt. I know how that feels."

"You didn't hurt me David. I honestly couldn't imagine you hurting anyone so for what it's worth – I believe you've changed."

"Thanks, Katherine. It means a lot to me. My heart's desire is for others to see me and know that I'm not that man who went to prison. I want my family to know that I've changed. I pray that one day Marcie will forgive me."

"Marcie. Who is Marcie?" Katherine looked at David waiting for him to respond.

David dropped his eyes and turned away from Katherine's gaze. He'd said more than he intended to say. Now, he'd have to talk about Marcie.

As soon as she had spoken, Katherine regretted it. She wished she would have just listened. "I'm sorry David. Now, I'm bringing back painful memories. How about this? - let's just count the stars for the remainder of our walk."

Katherine grabbed David's arm and leaned her head on his shoulder. "That's enough therapy for tonight. We'll continue tomorrow."

The only thing David really heard was the word tomorrow. Katherine wasn't running away. He couldn't believe it. He walked quietly feeling valued. Katherine valued their friendship enough not to run away. He smiled as he looked up at the stars. His fantasy was getting better day by day. He would enjoy it as long as possible. He realized it could end at any moment.

They walked for twenty minutes arm in arm before they ended up back in the neighborhood. As they neared the driveway, Katherine tugged on David's arm and he stopped just as she hoped.

"I still haven't told Aunt Jane and Uncle James about Justin."

David immediately responded, "And they won't hear about Justin from me."

Katherine smiled indicating she was pleased. "Thanks David. Your secret is safe with me as well."

Chapter 16

Marcie and Anthony

Marcie was startled by the phone ringing. She looked over at her clock it was nine forty five. She couldn't believe she'd slept that long.

"Hello." She spoke softly. It was probably obvious to whoever was calling that she had been sleeping.

"Good morning. May I speak to Marcie Rivera."

Marcie was startled by the male voice that certainly did not belong to Anthony. She quickly rubbed her eyes and sat up in the bed.

"This is Agent Winters with the US Marshall's office in Memphis. I've been assigned to apprehend David Rivera."

Marcie swallowed and whispered her response. "Yes, how can I help you?"

"Well ma'am we've gotten some information that may help us locate David. I wanted you to know that and I wanted to ask you if you have heard from him or if you had information that could helpful."

Now Marcie became nervous. She felt a flash of heat coming from her neck and rise to her cheeks. She honestly didn't want to cause David anymore trouble. She really wanted to move past this horrible season in her life. She spoke slowly and deliberately searching for the right words. She couldn't lie, but she didn't want to say anything that would make his situation worse.

"Agent Winters, I have no idea where David is. I hope that he is hundreds of miles away from me. I did see him, but it was months ago."

"Where did you see him?"

"He just showed up at my front door. I didn't know it was him until I opened the door. By then, it was too late. Fortunately, all he wanted to do was apologize to me. A friend of mine drove up and he ran off."

"Have you seen or heard from him since that time?"

"No I haven't."

"Well, Mrs. Rivera I hope that before long I'll be calling you to let you know he's back in custody. Until then I'm going to ask you to continue to be cautious and please call me if he attempts to contact you in anyway. Do you have something so that you can write down my name and contact information?"

"Hold on for one moment please. Okay, I'm ready."

"My name is Agent Lawrence Winters. I am at the Memphis field office and my number is 901628..."

Marcie felt like she was having an out of body experience as she copied the information. For several weeks she had slept without the fear of David knocking on her door. Now, she felt as if he could be right outside. As she hung up the phone, she looked at the clock. She didn't have any time to worry about David right now. Anthony and the girls would be knocking on the door in less than an hour. They would be going to a late breakfast and then school shopping for the girls.

She hurried to the closet and grabbed the clothes she'd picked out the day before. A bubble bath seemed like a great way to start the morning. She grabbed a bottle of her aromatherapy stress relief bubble bath and started the water. As she poured, she inhaled. She needed to relax. Twenty minutes later she emerged from her bath feeling refreshed and ready to shop. Anthony and the girls arrived on time as usual. Maxine and Mavis were full of energy and requests. They each had a list of things they couldn't live without and questions about everything else in sight.

Anthony noticed as soon as Marcie came to the door that something wasn't right. He wasn't sure what it was and he didn't want to risk bringing it up in front of the girls. He decided to do his best to make this shopping trip as short as possible so that he could have time to figure out what was bothering Marcie.

Marcie was happy to have the girls to keep her mind occupied. They tried on dresses, shorts, jeans, shoes and every other piece of clothing insight. By the end of the shopping spree, Anthony was begging for mercy.

"Okay ladies it's time to go home. I think you have everything on your list plus several other things."

Anthony was surprised that the girls offered no resistance. It wasn't long after they started their trip that Maxine and Mavis were asleep in the back seat. Anthony decided to use this as an opportunity to see what Marcie was thinking about.

"Hey, what are you thinking about over there? You've been distracted all day."

Marcie glanced back at the girls in the back seat to confirm they were asleep. "I got a phone call this morning from the US Marshall's office. An Agent Winters called to see if I'd heard from David and if I knew where he might be. I was startled awake by the phone, and talking about David always leaves me with an uneasy feeling. That's it." She let out a small sigh, "I just wish this would all end."

"Why didn't you tell me? I wouldn't have put you through the chaos of shopping with the girls." Anthony looked disappointed.

"I wanted to go. We had been planning this all week. Besides, I needed to be with you guys. I certainly didn't need to sit in that apartment and think about this. Agent Winters thinks that he has a good idea of where David is and expects to have him back in custody soon."

"That's great!" Noticing her expression, he then asked," Isn't it? You don't look like you're happy about that."

"I can't explain how I'm feeling. David was right in front of me and he didn't attempt to hurt me. He apologized and this time it was different. I think it's possible that he's changed. I wouldn't bet my life on it, but as long as he stays away from me I don't care where he is. I really just want all of this to be over."

"And it will be Marcie. David may have changed, but he still has to serve his time. Forgiveness doesn't always nullify the consequences. If you forgive, you release yourself and that person to move forward in peace, but sometimes forgiveness still requires the person to suffer the consequences of his behavior. David is going to have consequences for what he did to you and for escaping. I'm glad you have forgiven him. Once he is in custody again you will feel even better. Don't feel guilty about any of this. David is totally responsible for whatever happens to him. He violated the law. He decided to run instead of accepting the consequences of his behavior. You are not responsible. I need you to understand that and to believe it."

"I know," she said quietly. However, in her mind, she couldn't help feeling that David had changed.

Chapter 18

David

Katherine was awakened by the sound of voices outside her window. The voices seemed closer than they should have been. She was home alone and no one should have been in the yard. She quickly exited the bed and looked out the window. She was startled to see several men in dark clothing. They were surrounding the Mercys' house. Then, she saw him and her heart dropped. David was being escorted around the side of the house in handcuffs. In a matter of seconds, Katherine was dressed and running out the front door towards David.

She stopped dead in her tracks when she realized the men yelling - "Stop" had their guns pointed at her. She burst into tears.

"What's going on? What did he do? Can I talk to him? Please can I talk to him?"

The man nearest her began to speak. "Ma'am, what's your name?"

Katherine wiped her tears and answered slowly. "Katherine."

He continued, "Katherine, we're going to lower our weapons, but you have to stay on that porch. I'm going to need you to turn around and face the wall. We are US Marshalls and your neighbor is in our custody. Do you understand what I'm saying Katherine?"

Katherine couldn't speak so she shook her head and turned to face the wall.

The agent approached Katherine and spoke something to her softly. Katherine nodded and raised her hands. He checked her pockets and then motioned to the other officers to lower their weapons. He then asked Katherine to sit down.

"Ma'am, I'm going to allow you to speak to your neighbor, but you must remain calm."

The officer motioned for Katherine to walk with him. She moved slowly still in shock. She couldn't believe what she'd run into trying to escape her own troubles. As she approached the car, David looked away as if he was collecting his thoughts. He took a deep breath and then looked back at Katherine. Before he could speak, Katherine began, "David I believe you changed. You have to face the consequences of your actions, but that doesn't mean you haven't changed. I believe you and I'll be here when you come back."

Tears filled David's eyes and he found it impossible to speak. He nodded his head, attempting to turn away from her, so she couldn't see the tears rolling down his cheek. The officer who had been holding Katherine about a foot away from the car released her. Katherine immediately reached towards the car through the open window. She wiped the tears from his face and promised not to run away. "You've been a good friend to me David. I won't run away."

The officer gently pulled Katherine away from the car. She felt an arm around her shoulders and looked up and saw

Grayson Mercy. He escorted her back to his porch and they both watched as the car with David drove down the street followed by several other black SUVs.

Katherine felt the warmth of tears on her cheek. She felt as if she'd lost her best friend. Once the cars were out of sight Grayson walked Katherine into the kitchen where Grace was waiting. She was preparing breakfast. As Katherine walked in, she turned to address her. "Katherine, I'm cooking breakfast. I know you probably don't want to eat, but we need to eat something before we leave. It's going to be a long day." Katherine looked confused. "The officer said that after David was processed in they would allow us to have a brief visit."

Katherine was excited about seeing David again, but she still felt empty inside. "Thanks Mrs. Mercy, but I'm not hungry."

"You will eat something. I have fruit and homemade biscuits. You chose."

The drive to Memphis was quiet except for the soft jazz Grayson always played when he drove. Katherine had no idea what she'd say to David. She didn't feel like there was anything left to say, but she still wanted to see him. She believed he had changed.

David, Katherine, Grayson and Grace

As they walked into the detention center, Katherine felt as if her knees would buckle. She really wasn't prepared for the strip search/pat down they had to go through before they were allowed to proceed inside. As she put back on her shoes and her bra, she wondered if this was a good idea. The woman officer who checked her was cordial, but Katherine still felt violated. As she walked through the bars to the waiting area, she realized that David's past must have caught up to him. She wondered if his family member had filed charges and he'd been on the run this whole time. Now, she really didn't know what to say. When Mr. Mercy suggested he and Mrs. Mercy would go in first, she was relieved.

David was relieved but he was still on edge. He wondered who was here to see him so quickly. Perhaps the officers had notified Marcie and he was about to face her and her new boyfriend. He began to pray for God to give him the words. This was his chance to finally apologize and he didn't want to mess it up. When the doors opened, he was once again relieved. It was Grayson and Grace Mercy, but then his relief gave way to anxiousness when he realized the Mercys knew the truth. What had they come to say? The sound of Grayson's voice immediately relaxed David. He realized that nothing had changed. Grayson still had a protective, fatherly tone as he spoke.

"David, are you ok? Grace and I both want you to know that we are here to support you."

David raised his head and looked at both Grayson and Grace with sheer awe in his gaze. "Why? What have I done to deserve your loyalty?"

Grayson spoke slowly, but with authority. "You've done nothing to not deserve it David. You are just like our son."

David smiled. He felt like Mr. Grayson was a father to him but Grayson looked at him as if he wasn't finished. David realized there was more.

"Our son Michael was a lot like you. He wasn't our birth child, but we adopted him. He left home when he was seventeen. He changed his name, but we figured out where he was and kept up with him through some of our friends. He was determined to find his biological family, which he did. Unfortunately, after meeting them, he didn't adjust too well. He turned to alcohol and drugs. We even heard that he was abusive to some of the women he dated. He died a few years ago in a car accident. We never had the chance to reconcile with him. I blamed myself for not going after him when he first left home. We had one fight about a party where his friends were smoking marijuana. I don't even think he was involved, but I was hard on him. Apparently too hard, because he left and I insisted we not go after him. You reminded us so much of him and I've been determined since I met you to help you if you wanted help. Do you remember what I told you the first day we met?"

David smiled and looked over at Mrs. Mercy remembering how protective Grayson had been of his wife. David nodded.

Grayson continued, "You didn't violate our agreement and I've seen how you've worked to do better. We will do whatever we can to help you David. In our eyes, you are just like our son and we won't turn our backs on you regardless of what is going on with you now."

David was humbled. "Thank you. Thank you too Mrs. Mercy. You two have really changed my life. I know I have to serve my time, but you have taught me so much about being a man Grayson. I didn't get that from my own father. You showed me how to love a woman. I've watched the way you care for Grace. I hope that one day I'll be able to have a love like that."

Grace spoke for the first time. "Speaking of love – Katherine is with us. She's waiting to see you."

David's eyes lit up. "She came."

Grayson smiled, "Yes she did. Don't try to tell her everything at once. Just say the important stuff. You won't have a lot of time. Make it count."

David nodded. Once again Mr. Grayson was acting like a father speaking to his son – giving him exactly what he needed.

David was nervous as he waited for Katherine to come in, but seeing the nervous look on her face calmed his fears.

"Thanks for coming Katherine. I didn't expect you to come."

Katherine was still shaken from the security search. Even though she only had to take off her bra, the idea of being patted down did not sit well with her. She felt bad for David. It sounded like he was going to be in jail for a long time. She didn't really understand how the man in front of her could have committed the crimes he was found guilty of. She was glad that touching wasn't allowed because it was going to take her a while to reconcile this in her head. A part of her wanted to hug David and tell him things would be ok. Another part of her just wanted to run.

"Katherine, I honestly don't know what to say. You didn't run. Thanks. I could use a friend."

"David, I want to hear your side of the story. I know there's not enough time now but I want to hear from you and I won't run even if it scares me. I know enough about you to believe that you have changed."

"Thanks. That's the least I can do. I hope that time will be on my side and you won't get tired of waiting. Thanks for believing in me. Thanks for coming."

The guard signaled to David that time was up. Katherine got up hesitantly. As she walked out the door, she looked back at David. "I'll write you back David if you write."

"Count on it." David replied. He couldn't believe it. He'd never had support before. Having three people see him at his worst behind bars and commit to standing by him was beyond his comprehension. He knew without a doubt that there was a god and God was showing him unmerited favor.

Chapter 19

Marcie, David, Grace, Grayson, and Katherine

David was prepared to spend the next twenty-five years in jail. His attorney had warned that a sentence less than that would be nothing short of a miracle. This wasn't a case of guilt or innocence but a matter of sentencing. David had already been found guilty. He hoped for mercy, but he realized he'd violated the law on multiple occasions. His cowardly escape would not be overlooked.

David stood beside his attorney and watched as the judge entered the courtroom. He felt like he was on an island. Not until he turned to reach for his seat did he realize Marcie was present in the court room. His heart dropped. All hope of this being an uneventful sentencing proceeding was gone. Katherine was there and she'd hear what he'd actually done to Marcie how he'd ruined her life. He'd have to relive it all again and this side of him certainly would make Katherine run.

David dropped his head and again whispered a prayer. Prayer had become an essential part of his life. He couldn't be angry with Marcie for showing up. He'd ruined her life and she'd never lied on him. Everything she said in court in the past had been the truth. It was just so hard to accept that he had been so out of control.

He quickly made up his mind to take his punishment like a man. He held his head up and took one final glance at Katherine. She smiled back and he could feel warmth throughout his body. He knew that after today Katherine would never see him the same way again. This was the seed he'd sewn. He had to face the consequences of his rebellious behavior.

First to speak on David's behalf was Mr. Grayson. He spoke of David like a prodigal son. He talked about David rededicating his life to Christ, his participation in the men's ministry at the church and his work with mentoring young men in the community.

"My wife and I have grown to love David as if he were our own son. We realize that he has done some horrible things. He wasn't himself. He's repented and his actions are proof that he has truly changed. He has been alcohol and drug free since I met him months ago. David is a part of our family now and I think that with the right support he'll continue to do the right thing. We believe in him. His heart is bent towards God and he desires to do good and not evil."

David's eyes filled with tears as he listened to Mr. Grayson. He'd referred to him as a part of his family. He wasn't ashamed of him. Hearing Mr. Grayson repeat the things he'd said to him when he was first arrested was almost overwhelming. No one had ever shown him that type of loyalty except Marcie and he'd ruined that relationship. He concentrated really hard on preventing the tears that had formed in his eyes from rolling down his cheeks. He pushed his head back and waited for a moment hoping to counteract the effects of gravity.

Next, Ms. Peters from the homeless shelter took the stand. David was surprised even more. She spoke of how respectful and hardworking Donald (David) had been while he was living in the shelter. She added, "I can't imagine what he has done to warrant him to be locked up. I just know he is an outstanding young man. He worked hard and was always willing to help others in need. He's welcome in my shelter any time."

David listened as Katherine and then Grace spoke on his behalf. He wasn't sure what would happen but to him just having this many people speak on his behalf was nothing short of a miracle.

At the end of Grace's testimony, the judge looked to the audience and addressed Marcie. "Mrs. Rivera, would you like to address the court?"

Marcie had been stunned listening to all of the favorable comments of David's new friends. Inside she couldn't help but smile. They had met the David she fell in love with. All was not lost. There was another David inside. She wasn't as crazy as she had felt after all.

Marcie felt Anthony reach for her hand. She realized the judge was waiting for her to respond. "Yes sir, I would."

"Very well then, we will take a ten minute recess and give you a few moments to collect your thoughts."

Marcie rose with the rest of the people in the court, but her mind was miles away. She realized that what she was about to say in court in front of all of these witnesses would seem crazy, but she had to speak her heart. She was the one that had to sleep at night.

When the court reconvened, Marcie kept her eyes focused on the judge. This wasn't going to be easy but it had to be done. After taking her place at the podium, Marcie positioned herself so that she could avoid eye to eye contact with David. "Good morning. My name is Marie Rivera. I came here today to remind the court of what an awful thing my ex-husband did to me. I came here to speak up for the victim I had become. I came here to speak up for the many women who have lost their voice due to domestic violence. I expected to be the only voice you heard and I knew what I had to do, but somewhere between the time I got up this morning and right now I realized that this proceeding today is about much more than just me and the pain I experienced. Today is about healing and moving forward. As I listened to each of David's new friends speak of him, I realized they met the man I married. Somewhere along the way things went wrong and he betrayed me in the worst way. He nearly took my life, but God did not allow that. God gave me another chance to live – to love. He gave me a chance to heal, move forward with my life and most of all to forgive. I believe that my ex-husband has changed. I believe he truly understands the dangers of using alcohol and drugs. I believe he deserves another chance to live and to love. He deserves a chance to move forward with his life." Marcie paused and then looked directly at David. "Your honor, I'm not here to demand the maximum sentence. I'll be fine with whatever sentence you impose. I chose to forgive and that means moving forward wishing David Rivera nothing but the best of what God has in store for him."

David could no longer hold back his tears. His prayers had been answered. Marcie seemed open to forgiving him and that meant more to him than anything in the world. He felt liberated.

As soon as Marcie reached her seat, the judge indicated he was ready to impose the sentence. "David Rivera your demeanor in court today, as well as, those that have spoken on your behalf has convinced me that your actions against your ex-wife were driven by your addiction. I am convinced that as long as you remain sober, you will not pose any further threat to your ex-wife and will remain a productive citizen. I thereby sentence you to time served for the assault against Marcie Rivera, six months for your escape, mandatory drug rehab until a licensed counselor deems you have satisfied the program requirements and seven years' probation to begin once you have completed your prison sentence. I hope that you will not disappoint all of these people who have placed their trust in you- God speed."

The three bangs of the judge's gavel brought a gasp of relief from the audience. David turned to see Katherine. Her eyes too were full of tears. She smiled and mouthed to him *"I'm not running."* David's eyes lit up and he mouthed back, *"Thank you."*

He also saw Marcie moving quickly to get out of the court room followed closely by Anthony. He wanted to thank her, but he knew this wasn't the right time. He looked back at his attorney. "Well, I'd say we just experienced a miracle." He extended his hand then reached out to give his attorney a quick embrace. "Thank you. I think I just got my life back."

David's attorney stunned replied, "I believe you did. Indeed this was miraculous. I wish you all the best."

Chapter 20

Anthony and Marcie

The car was quiet except for the voice on the radio. Marcie wasn't sure what to say. She knew that Anthony was upset because she had testified for David. Well, she knew that he had barely said two words to her since she told him she was going to the hearing. Besides insisting he was going with her, he hadn't said much.

In an attempt to see how Anthony would respond Marcie asked, "Are you hungry? I'm starving. I didn't eat breakfast."

Anthony responded slowly as if he was considering his answer. "Actually, I am. Would you like to stop and get something or would you rather I cook something when we get home."

"Well, if we stop it will give us some time to talk. I can't help but feel like you'd like to get some things off your chest." Marcie encouraged Anthony to speak up.

Anthony took advantage of the moment. "I've been thinking a lot lately and I have some things to share but it's not what you think. I'm not mad at you. At first I was. Then, I was more hurt by your loyalty to David. I realized that I was being self-centered and a little jealous. I had to step back and look at the full picture. You have gone from being a terrified woman to a courageous woman of God. I can only imagine how hard it was for you to put aside your own feelings and forgive David for all of the evil he did to you. And then what really changed my heart was when I realized that your willingness to forgive David and your new found level of courage could have only come from God."

"You have grown so much in Christ and I have the privilege of calling you mine. So what I really want to say to you Marcie is that I'm sorry. I'm sorry for behaving like a spoiled, jealous boyfriend. You are a strong and courageous woman. You've shown that to everyone who dares to look beyond the surface. I'm proud to have you on my arm. I'd love to take you out to eat or cook for you while you relax. It's been quite a day so whatever you'd prefer."

"I couldn't have done any of this without your support Anthony. You have been my lifeline and I truly appreciate you just being there when I needed someone I could depend on. You taught me how to trust again. You made me feel safe. You shared your love and I just soaked it all in. You gave me the desire to move forward with my life. You never wavered even when I tried to push you away. Thank you for being willing to stand by my side through all of this. I think I'd rather eat at home. A glass of lemonade on the deck sounds good."

Anthony was beaming inside. Had he heard her correctly? Marcie had said "home" and her apartment didn't have a deck. "I'll put some steak and chicken on the grill and we can watch the sun go down."

"I can't think of anything I'd rather do. I feel like I have been born again. This must be what they mean in that song: *Joy, Joy, God's great joy – Joy, joy down in my soul. Sweet beautiful, soul saving joy - Oh! Joy, joy in my soul.* Today is a great day Anthony. It couldn't be better. Thanks."

Chapter 21

David

David walked into his cell and dropped down on the hard mattress. He couldn't believe how today's court appearance had gone. God had truly moved mountains. He couldn't believe how truly blessed he was to have so many people speak up for him. Katherine, the Graysons, even Marcie. Katherine had even contacted the shelter director, Ms. Peters, on his behalf.

So many things had worked in his favor. He would be serving a six month sentence for his escape. After listening to the testimony and reviewing the case history especially the indiscretions surrounding the original trial, the judge decided to reduce the original sentence to time served and place him on probation. In six months he would be a free man again. This time he would not have to worry about "getting caught."

Marcie was ok with it too. She'd said that after listening to all of the other testimony, she was convinced he had changed and she'd forgiven him. As long as he didn't try to contact her she was ok with him going forward with his life. The judge had issued a permanent restraining order, as well as, participation in a substance dependence recovery program once he was released. His probation would begin upon completion of his sentence and last for seven years.

David leaned back and began to sob. He couldn't believe how fortunate he was. He couldn't believe God had shown him so much mercy and showered him with grace. This must be what it felt like to "born again."

He wiped away his tears and looked around for paper and a pencil. He sat down and began to write. He spent hours putting together his thoughts. Moments after he finished writing, it was time for dinner.

Even though David knew the food wouldn't be spectacular, he walked out of his cell with a smile on his face and pep in his step. One hundred and seventy nine more dinners and he'd be a free man.

Chapter 22

Anthony and Marcie

Anthony could not sit still. He walked from his living room to the deck for almost an hour before he decided to turn on some jazz to try and calm down. He picked up the box that contained the ring. He only hoped things would go as planned and most importantly - Marcie would say "yes".

Anthony reached for the phone. It seemed as if the call was taking forever to go through. "Monique?"

"Hi Anthony."

"Do you have everything in place? I need you to have Marcie at Maxwell's at six, not a minute early and not a minute late."

"Relax Anthony. It's taken care of. She'll be there. Do you have everything you need? Kent will be at Maxwell's at 5:30 to meet you with the balloons and cake. Have you ordered the flowers?"

"Yes, I've ordered bouquets for each table red, white and pink. I picked up my tux yesterday and had a dress sent over to Marcie as a surprise. I told her I wanted us to dress in the same colors for the party. She didn't act as if she suspected anything. I'm so excited I can hardly sit still. I can't focus. I keep going over my words. I want everything to be perfect."

Anthony paused and took a deep breath. "I never thought I'd be doing this again, but I can't imagine anything else I'd rather do."

"I think you've made a wise choice Anthony. Marcie and you make a great couple." Monique replied.

"Thanks Monique. I don't know if I would have been courageous enough to pursue this relationship without the support of you and Kent. You guys are wonderful."

"You're family Anthony – anything for you and the girls. You can always count on us being there."

"Thanks Monique. I'll see you later."

Marcie

The day seemed to be going by so slowly. Marcie was excited about participating in the family celebration. Anthony had written an award winning article and he'd been offered a position as the features editor of a prominent newspaper in the city. He'd worked so hard and been through so much. Marcie could not believe how strong he was. He wasn't bitter at all. It was no secret how much he loved Rachel, yet he hadn't allowed losing her to infect his heart. That's what she loved about him most. He was kindhearted and strong.

She hoped that tonight's celebration would be perfect. Anthony seemed excited about it too. He'd purchased her a dress so that they could coordinate their apparel for the evening. She always enjoyed spending time with Monique and Kent. Monique had been so helpful. She'd helped her choose a nice bracelet for Anthony and was going to pick her up for the dinner. Everything was set and she couldn't wait until her workday was over. She was anticipating good food and lots of laughs.

Marcie and Monique

Anthony, Kent, Mavis, Maxine

Monique smiled inside and out as Marcie walked outside and got into the car. Marcie looked stunning. Anthony was going to lose his mind when he saw her in that dress. She looked just like she'd stepped off of a fashion magazine cover.

"Hi Marcie – Girl, you look fantabulous."

"Thanks Monique. I have been excited about tonight all day."

"Well, you are dressed for the occasion and I expect we will have a wonderful evening."

Monique and Marcie spent the rest of their drive catching up. They had just finished Monique's latest story about the girls when they pulled into the parking lot at Maxwell's. On cue, Anthony walked up to the passenger side door and offered Marcie his arm. He looked remarkably handsome.

He talked softly as they walked towards the restaurant. "Do you remember our first date? I was so nervous."

"I was too." Marcie replied smiling.

As she finished her statement, she looked up and saw Maxine and Mavis. They were dressed in beautiful purple dresses similar to her own. Each of them was holding a bouquet of roses. As Marcie and Anthony reached the door Maxine and Mavis ran towards them. "Hi Ms. Marcie these are for you."

Marcie could not hide her surprise. She realized things were not as they had seemed. She'd been had. She looked up at Anthony for an explanation, but he only smiled.

Maxine and Mavis continued. "Ms. Marcie tonight is a very special night for all of us. Do you like our dresses? Daddy picked them."

"I do." Marcie replied. "You two are so beautiful. I need to take a picture before we leave."

"We will take lots of pictures. Cousin Kent brought his big camera." Mavis replied.

Just as Mavis finished her sentence she realized that there had been flashes of light going off around her. She looked to find Kent with his "big camera" pointed at her and the girls. She looked at Anthony once again. "What is this?"

"It's a special night babe and I wanted it to be as special for you as it is for me."

Marcie could have melted in his arms. He always made her feel special, but she couldn't help but wonder what else he had planned. Two dozen roses, Kent taking pictures, curbside service from Monique...it seemed over the top even for Anthony. He'd never involved others before. He must really be excited about his new position.

"I know that you thought tonight was just about my promotion, but since I hate to be the center of attention I decided to include you and the girls. Just like the girls said – tonight is going to be a special night for all of us."

Marcie smiled, "You are some kind of guy. That's why I love you."

"Good, my night is special already. The woman I love is on my arm and she has openly declared her love for me. I have Mavis, Maxine and rest of the people important to me. Let's enjoy this."

Marcie smiled and followed Anthony's lead. Anthony seated her at the table and walked around to sit in front of her. She realized almost immediately that this was the exact table where they had their first date. She wouldn't have to sneak off to the bathroom to call Monique because she was seated at the table beside her with Kent and their children. With that exception this was a recreation of that first night. It seemed like decades had passed. That one time stranger had proven to be a man she could trust. A man who'd do anything to make sure she was taken care of.

Marcie smiled even harder. She had trusted her instincts about Anthony and she had been right.

The night seemed perfect. Kent snapped photos with his "big camera" throughout the night, but other than that everyone seemed to be making a point of staying away.

Anthony was confident as usual but he also seemed anxious. He spent the night reminding Marcie of how their first few months together were. They were in the middle of remembering his first surprise visit when the waitress walked up with a "to go" tray.

Marcie snickered because as she looked at both of their plates she realized there was nothing "to go". They'd quietly talked and unlike their first date finished the entire meal.

Anthony smiled and reached for the tray. The waitress walked away and Anthony stood up. Immediately Kent began snapping pictures again. She looked over to see everyone staring. Marcie looked back at Anthony, she realized he was kneeling in front of her with the opened "to go" tray in one hand. In the tray she saw it, an open ring box and the most beautiful diamond ring she'd ever seen.

Anthony began to speak. "Marcie you've taught me so much about faith, strength and courage. I have fallen in love with the woman you are inside and out. I want to spend the rest of my life learning from you and experiencing all the joys of life with you. Will you marry me?"

It seemed as if all eyes were on her. Marcie looked up and realized that everyone in the restaurant was looking on – waiting for her response. She then noticed that a lot of the faces looking on were familiar. She looked back at Anthony, searching for the right words.

"Anthony, you are perfect. Not in the eyes of man, but in my eyes you are perfect for me. You have encouraged me, supported me and protected me. I'm so nervous right now everyone is staring at us, but I do know what I would be a fool to pass up a chance of a lifetime. I would be honored to be your wife. Yes!"

Anthony moved closer, removing the ring from the box and placing it on Marcie's finger. He then kissed her softly – first on her ring finger then her hand, then her forehead, and finally passionately on her lips.

Their embrace was interrupted by cheers and clapping from the patrons and wait staff of the restaurant. Mavis and Maxine walked to the table. This time each of them held a half of a dozen red roses.

"These are from daddy, Ms. Marcie. We are going to have lots of fun together."

Marcie smiled and gave the girls a big hug. "We sure are."

Chapter 23

Marcie and Anthony

Marcie looked out over the horizon. She loved sitting on the deck in the evening. It was always so quiet and peaceful. Anthony had done a wonderful job choosing them a home. As she looked out into the darkness, she whispered a prayer to God.

Dear Lord,

Thank you for all that you have done in my life. I don't want to even think about how bad this could have been. You spared my life. It could have ended and I would have never accepted you as my Savior. I wouldn't have enjoyed the certainty of knowing that I will have eternal life. I'm living an abundant life now because of your grace and mercy. Thank you Lord.

Marcie looked up to find Anthony standing by her side with a cup of tea in one hand and an envelope in the other. He smiled at her and handed her the tea.

"You made it home early tonight. I thought me and the girls would get here first."

"I left early today. I wanted to get home and just relax. I've been sitting here thanking God for his grace and mercy."

"I see you've already finished dinner. I thought you might like some tea to help you relax. I also wanted to share something with you. I received this at work today. It contains two letters. One is addressed to you. The other is addressed to me. They are from David. I thought you should read them."

"Why now? Why is he trying to contact me and why you? It's been almost two years."

"I think you should read them Marcie. Both letters are in the envelope. I'm going to go inside and get the girls ready for dinner. I'll give you some time alone."

Anthony kissed Marcie and walked back in the door.

Marcie picked up the envelope and removed the letters. The first one was addressed to Anthony. She braced herself and began to read.

Anthony,

I'm writing you because I saw the notice of your marriage to Marcie in the paper. It's taken me six months to sit down and write this letter to you. I screwed up man. I know that and I'm sure you do to. I wanted to congratulate you on marrying one of the strongest women I know. I did everything I could to destroy her, but she didn't give up. You're lucky man. I am sorry for all of the pain I caused Marcie. This is the last time you'll hear from me, but I wanted to apologize to Marcie and tell her how she really has changed my life for the better.

I saw you in court with Marcie. I recognized the anger in your eyes when you stared at me from across the room. I could also see the love you have for Marcie. I hope that you will cherish her and take care of her. She deserves that.

I'm sending my letter to you, because you are responsible for protecting her now. If you think that what I've written will cause Marcie more pain please destroy it. If not, I'd appreciate the opportunity to tell her thanks and to apologize one last time.

I am truly a new man and I have Marcie to thank for that. She showed me what unconditional love was truly about. I wish you a lifetime full of Jesus' joy.

David,

"The New Man"

P.S. God blessed me. He was merciful and gracious. I owe the credit for my second chance at happiness to Marcie and her willingness to forgive me. She gave me the courage to try and forgive myself which allowed me to try love again.

Marcie picked up her cup of tea, took a sip and then looked out into the darkness. She couldn't believe these were the words of David. He used the name of Jesus and said he had been blessed by God. This was miraculous. She only hoped he was sincere, but that wasn't her call to make. She whispered a prayer and prepared to read the second letter.

Marcie was surprised to see that her letter was dated almost two years earlier (August 14, 2011). In fact, if memory served her correctly the letter was written on the day David was sentenced for his escape. Again she embraced herself and began to read.

Dear Marcie,

I don't know if I'll ever get the courage to mail this letter to you, but I have to try. I must say to you again, I'm sorry. I hurt you physically and emotionally. I am guilty of nothing less.

You have every right to wish me evil, but you don't. I can't say that I even understand that. I watched you as you testified today. I didn't see anger, hatred, or revenge. I saw compassion, concern and love. It was hard for me to believe you still had love for me after all I have done to you, but I saw it today.

I realized that only God could cause you to forgive me and speak on my behalf. You've changed so much. I saw Christ in you today Marcie and I realized that unconditional love does exist. God can heal all of our pain. He's healed you and I am thankful.

I know I did more damage to you Peaches, than I ever did good, but I see how God has worked in your life to heal the wounds I caused. I realize you'll always have scars and for this, I truly am sorry.

I want you to know that I have changed and watching you today has given me hope.

Thank you for forgiving me. I know that wasn't easy. You are a strong and beautiful woman. God has used you to answer my prayers.

Your forgiveness will not be wasted on me. I will make the most of my second chance. I wish you all the best Marcie. May God continue to protect, shield, and heal you. I didn't know how to show it, but I always loved you Peaches.

Always,

David

Marcie wiped the tears from the corners of her eyes. She wasn't sure how to feel, but she was certain that she had done the right thing – forgiving David. She walked over to the side of the deck and looked up at the moon. Moments later she felt the warmth of Anthony's arms engulf her. She leaned into his embrace.

"Are you okay babe?" Anthony questioned.

"I am now. What do you think about David's letters?"

"I tried not to think too hard. I prayed and decided you needed to read them for yourself. I hope that they will bring you closure."

"I've realized something after all I have been through. The pain I suffered at the hands of David, the fear I experienced while he was on the run, the protection I felt when you came into my life, and the confidence I gained after accepting Christ as my Savior-it took all of that to get me to this moment with you...I realized that love is a journey. I'm thankful to be traveling with you Anthony Ryan Monesta. I love you."

Epilogue

Katherine couldn't believe it. The day had finally come, but she wasn't sure she could go through with it. She knew David had changed. She believed it with all of her heart. He hadn't given her a reason to doubt that. She just couldn't get those pictures of what he had done to Marcie out of her head. How could the man she loved do that to another human being?

All kinds of images and thoughts raced through Katherine's mind as she stood at the entrance to the sanctuary. With both Grayson and her Uncle James by her side, there was no turning back now. God knew her heart. He knew David's heart. Katherine whispered a prayer as the music began.

Lord I'm depending on you to develop this marriage. I love David, the man you raised from the dead. I'm trusting you to lead and guide us as husband and wife. I'm believing you God.

David's eyes lit up as Katherine walked through the doors. He could not believe his good fortune. God truly was a loving and forgiving God capable of miracles. He stood as a living testimony, of the power of God. He looked over to the area reserved for his family. There wasn't an empty seat. He looked back at Katherine and for the first time since the day his sentence was set aside, he cried!

Discussion Questions for <u>Love is a Journey</u>

1. How does Anthony's loss of his first wife impact his relationship with Marcie?

2. How does Marcie's past relationship with David impact her relationship with Anthony?

3. Do you believe David's behavior while he was living at the shelter indicates he has made positive changes? Why or Why not?

4. What indicators are there that David may be making changes for the better once he takes the job with the Mercys?

5. What impact does the Mercys' decision to hire David have?

6. Katherine seemed to accept David for the person he had become as opposed to the person had been? What factors do you think contributed to her attitude towards David?

7. Marcie changed her attitude towards David. What factors do you think contributed to this change?

8. Anthony decided to share David's letters with Marcie instead of destroying them. Do you think this was the right thing to do? Why or why not?

9. How is unconditional love expressed by the characters: Anthony and Marcie?

10. What role does forgiveness play in the lives of Marcie and David? What is the positive impact on each of them?

God is With Me

When I feel alone convinced that the snare of the
enemy looms overhead,

I must not give up. I must not fear because the truth
has already been said clearly written for all to hear.
God is with me.

And though the dangers seem to be countless in
number, my mind is overwhelmed and has begun to
wonder, I will press on. I will believe what my God
has declared, because God is with me.

Today is a new day and my victory is guaranteed
because God is with me.

KIMBERLYN S. ALFORD

I've Been This Way Before

I've been this way before. Thought I wouldn't come back anymore.

Yet here I am again. Praying that it's all a part of God's divine plan.

It hurts no less.

Here I am - yet another test.

All I know to do is trust and lean on you.

You've never let me down. Your love is my crown.

I'm never alone it's true.

Even though this all seems new.

I've been this way before.

It's not as bad as it seems.

KIMBERLYN S. ALFORD

What's Next?

Avoiding it won't change a thing,

It's time to discover what's next.

You've done all that can be done.

At this level you faced challenges and mastered each one.

It's time to discover what's next.

Close your eyes and bow your head.

Listen for his voice and be by the Spirit led.

It's time to discover what's next.

KIMBERLYN S. ALFORD